THE FLYING BOY

OF CALHOUN COUNTY, TENNESSEE

A TALE FROM THE FRINGE OF REALITY

BY DAVID WALLECHINSKY

DEDICATION

This story is dedicated to Elijah and Aaron, carrying on the family tradition of searching for the odd, the unusual and the insightful.

CHAPTER 1

TWO SECONDS WITH GOD

My search for the flying boy of Calhoun County, Tennessee, was more important to me than all the other adventures I have written about or anything else that has happened to me since I was a little girl, for that matter. To understand why, you have to go back to the abductees' convention in San Francisco.

I make my living writing a column for the *New York Insider*, a weekly newspaper that began in the 1960s as a radical "underground" paper, but soon grew a fat belly, espousing its own cultural dogmas—smug, vaguely left-wing versions of the "establishment" media it once opposed.

My column, which appears bi-weekly, is called "The Fringe of Reality." It is my job to track down and expose strange tales and weird stories. One week I write about a bleeding statue of Jesus in a church in Presidio, Texas, another week a man in Brooklyn who died when an Australian Aborigine pointed a stick at him, and another week a nine-year-old boy in Logan County, Illinois, who claimed to have been grabbed by a huge bird that carried him through the air for fifty yards and then dropped him in a haystack.

For the first few months of writing my column I stayed away from UFO stories because it was such an overworked field. But then I hit on the angle that would lead to one of my biggest successes: a three-day-long abductees' convention. Abductees, not satisfied with merely *seeing* beings from outer space, claim to have been kidnapped by aliens. No less than 200 of these stalwarts from twelve countries gathered at a Ramada Inn in San Francisco, a city so blasé that the local newspapers gave the convention about as much space as a high school reunion.

Spending three days at a Ramada Inn with 200 abductees was like, dare I say it, stepping into another world. What a cast of characters!

There was Ryne Huey, a wide-eyed blond in his mid-twenties. He told me about the time he was returning home from his girlfriend's house in rural Alabama. One moment he was driving along, listening to the Cowsills singing "Captain Sad and His Ship of Fools," the next moment he was strapped naked to a table of cold leather, bright lights shining in his face, being probed and prodded by beings with one large eye and no mouth. Then he was back in his car again. The Cowsills were gone and his radio was set to a black hip hop station he hadn't known existed.

Fanny Blunk was so fat below the waist that she had to heave herself forward one leg at a time just to move. Fanny claimed to have been snatched out of her car while driving on a lonely highway, transported to a spaceship parked in a field and repeatedly violated by three-foot-tall aliens with elongated heads, block-shaped penises, and antennae coming out of their brains. As I said in my article, "Abductees: Take Them, Please," "No one but a three-foot-tall alien with an elongated head, a block-shaped penis, and antennae coming out of his brain would even *think* of violating Fanny Blunk."

Harry Philibert, a disturbingly normal forty-six-year-old accountant from Kettering, Ohio, had been abducted every 343 days for the past eight years. He gave me an insight into the psychological challenges involved in being an abductee. Not only did friends not believe what happened to you, but "No one believes you!" I shook my head in disbelief when Harry shared this with me. I think I even said, "Aren't people something?"

I attended workshops on "Dressing for an Expected Abduction" and "Increasing Recollections of Abduction Experiences without the Aid of Hypnosis." There was also a debate as to whether Alien Abductors are cruel, rubber-skinned villains who examine and violate their victims without remorse or whether they are benevolent creatures who want to befriend Earthlings and help them.

At an after-lunch seminar for "Women Who Have Engaged in Sexual Activities with Abductors," Carol Krmpetski, an attractive strawberry-blonde in her late-twenties, tearfully recounted having pleasureless sex with a short, gray-skinned creature with a mouth, but no lips.

"Sounds like my husband," said another, older woman, but the rest of the group was not amused.

My article on abductees appeared to rave reviews. Later it would haunt my conscience that I had publicly made fun of Fanny Blunk's appearance...but not yet. I received calls from *The New York Times* and *Rolling Stone* offering to hire me away from the *Insider*. I was even approached by an editor at Random House wanting to know if I had any book ideas. My boss, a pompous lecher named Lute Wisdom, was forced to give me a raise. This was heady stuff for a young woman barely out of college. I began fantasizing about winning a Pulitzer Prize, appearing on TV talk shows, being profiled in *People* magazine.

But in the midst of all this excitement, I was horrified to realize that part of me was actually envious of the very same abductees whom I had just mocked as weirdos. For days I walked around in a cloud, trying to pinpoint what it was that these oddballs had that I didn't. At last it came to me: no matter how crazy or terrified they had been, each of them had experienced a Defining Moment. Something unexpected had distracted them from the dullness of their lives and given them a purpose, even if that purpose was to tell anyone who would listen what had happened to them. I had no desire to be abducted myself, but I was reminded of an incident that had occurred when I was a little girl.

When I was born, my parents decided that my older brother and I should be raised in a small town and thus spared the ugliness of a big city like Durham, North Carolina. They bought a farmhouse outside the tiny, tobacco-farming community of Timberlake, my mother's hometown. This was before Timberlake became a popular bedroom community for people who worked in Durham. My memories of my earliest years are of utter bliss. Butterflies, drifting clouds, the smell of homemade bread. We never locked our doors in Timberlake. When I was a child, every cookie jar was open to me. If I was outside playing, I knew that I could walk up to any door and ask to use the bathroom or to pick something to eat from the garden. There were picnics and hay rides. In the summer we made the lightning bugs drunk with perfume; then we tied string around their tails and made lightning bug jewelry. Once a possum had her babies in our garbage can. I remember the smell of freshly plowed fields, of honeysuckle and magnolia, of spring rain. And the sounds of the frogs and the crickets before the rain. And the whistle of the cotton mill. And rabbits and squirrels and foxes, like in a fairy tale, and tadpoles in mud puddles and snakes in the creek.

When I was eight years old I began to notice that something was wrong. Gradually, sadly, I came to realize that my parents had almost nothing in common. My father, who was a psychology professor at the University of North Carolina, spent his spare time reading. He was a binge reader. Once he read all ninety-one of Balzac's novels—in chronological order. Another time he spent six months reading Eastern European short stories. My mother did not read books. She didn't read magazines or newspapers either. My father's other hobby was gardening. After work and on weekends he would spend every free daylight hour caressing his vegetable patch. Daddy really did have a green thumb. His tomatoes were sweeter than candy. Each bite of one of his carrots caused an explosion of taste. His pumpkins and zucchinis were twice as big as any sold in the stores. My mother refused to eat anything my father grew because he didn't use chemical pesticides. She would only eat store-bought produce and even then, she would only buy fruits and vegetables that were wrapped in plastic.

My mother's favorite foods were meat loaf, mashed potatoes and meringue. In other words, she preferred those foods you could beat and abuse until they were reduced to a smooth pulp. My father liked anything other than meat loaf, mashed potatoes or meringue. He was particularly fond of ethnic foods and would drive for twenty miles to try out a new Mexican or Thai restaurant. My mother refused to go with him.

My mother did have a hobby of her own: she collected reasons to hate people. Like any true collector, she cherished most those grudges that were hardest to find. If Ethel Barksdale appeared to slight her at the market one day, cutting off a session of chitchat because she had an appointment or because her bladder was full, my mother would hold this against Ethel Barksdale forever, even if Ethel Barksdale was blameless and the best of friends for the next twenty years—which she was. My father had only to say, "Wasn't that nice of Ethel to bake Suzy a cherry pie for her birthday?" and my mother would reply, "But you can't really trust Ethel as a friend.

One time in the market..."

Next door to us lived the Widow Marcus, as kind a person as ever inhabited the state of North Carolina. She baby-sat for free, took care of our house and pets when we went on vacation and listened patiently to the emotional outpourings of each member of our family. One time, about six months before my brother's first nervous breakdown, the Widow Marcus said to my mother, "Lucy, don't you think you should ease up a bit on Kyle?" Thereafter, whenever anyone praised an act of kindness by the Widow Marcus, my mother would launch into a bitter tirade about "that busybody who tried to tell me how to raise my own children."

Another thing my mother liked to do was watch television. My father's TV viewing was limited to the evening news and the occasional PBS documentary about the Civil Rights Movement or the Second World War. My mother, on the other hand, could always find something of interest to keep her company while she did her housework. In the early morning she watched Christian Aerobics, although she didn't do the exercises herself. Her favorite television personalities were the televangelists. She didn't care much for uplifting sermons, but when Pat Robertson or Jerry Falwell let loose with a vicious attack against some aspect of secular culture, she would smile contentedly. She leavened this cheery fare with Oprah Winfrey and Geraldo Rivera. Once I caught her watching Phil Donahue. She claimed she was just switching channels, but I knew she was lying.

My mother considered herself a devout Christian. I never saw her read the Bible, but she talked about God a lot and so did her mother, my Grandmother Farrell. This is what led to the incident I recalled after the abductees' convention.

My Grandmother Farrell always told me that God watches over the life of every person on Earth. My father was too tactful to dispute this openly, but he did take me aside and explain to me that any theory worth believing should stand up to examination. So one day, when I was ten years old, I put my grandmother's faith in God to the test. I reckoned that even God needed at least two seconds to study each person's life and put it in order. Certainly I would have been hurt if He devoted less time than that to my own life. I pulled out a piece of college-ruled notebook paper and made my calculations. Two seconds per person meant thirty people per minute. Sixty minutes in an hour meant 1,800 people per hour. Twenty-four hours in a day meant 43,200 people per day. Multiply that by 365 days for 15,768,000 people per year. Multiply that by seventy years, the average human life span, and it came to 1,103,760,000 people. Add eighteen leap year days per lifetime for an extra 777,600 people and a grand total of 1,104,537,600 people were looked after by God during an average lifetime. Since the population of the world was more than six billion and growing rapidly, God really had time to help only one out of six people.

I brought my calculations to Grandmother Farrell. She was not impressed. She explained, somewhat crossly, that God was omniscient and could look after all six billion people at once. I was not convinced. It looked like an ugly confrontation was about to take place. I imagined my grandmother complaining to my mother and my mother complaining to my father. My older brother and I would end up hiding and worrying about the muffled arguments that we were not supposed to hear.

But this time we were reprieved. My grandmother's stern expression suddenly gave way to beatific joy. She studied my calculations again and then exclaimed, "One billion, one hundred million: why, that's exactly how many Christians there are in the world!" She patted me on the head and added, "I guess you were right, after all, Suzy. God bless you."

Grandmother Farrell lived on this anecdote for years, as if I, her own granddaughter, had single-handedly and irrefutably proven the existence of God.

I, on the other hand, felt more concerned than ever. I became convinced that if I wasn't paying attention when God got around to my two seconds, this once-in-a-lifetime opportunity would be wasted. And I knew from my calculations that my two seconds could come at any time, not just morning, noon or night, but during childhood, middle age or, as my other grandmother, Watkins, liked to call them, "the years of complaining and forgetting."

So, for the rest of my childhood, no matter what I was doing, I never concentrated fully because a part of me was always looking out of the corner of my mind's eye, watching out for God.

When I went off to college in New York City, I became somewhat less vigilant, but even then, despite all the ugliness and cynicism I saw and felt, a part of me was still watching out, still waiting for my two seconds with God.

CHAPTER 2

ADVENTURES IN YOKELLAND

I graduated from the Columbia University Graduate School of Journalism in May 1999. As I was top of my class, everyone expected that I would go to work for *The New York Times* or *The Washington Post*. But I resented the assumption that my accomplishments had fated me to a certain path. So, to the surprise of my friends and to the dismay of my professors, I applied instead for a position at the *Insider*.

The editor of the *Insider*, the aforementioned Lute Wisdom, hired me immediately and tried me out at every beat in the city. Music concerts, political demonstrations, homeless shelters, ethnic enclaves; you name it, I covered it.

Then Lute decided to try an experiment. He gave me a roundtrip ticket to Bend, Oregon, and a motel reservation in nearby Prineville, and told me to write an article about Crook County, the only county in the United States that had always voted for the winner in presidential elections. For five days I wandered around Prineville and the surrounding countryside chatting up the locals and encouraging them to discuss their political beliefs. I was concerned not so much with for *whom* they were going to vote in the upcoming election, George W. Bush, Al Gore or Ralph Nader, as with the reasons behind their choices.

The results of my inquiry were appalling. The very first person I spoke with, a waitress in the motel restaurant, told me that she intended to vote for Bush because she still held it against the Democrats that Jimmy Carter had pardoned Richard Nixon. When I politely explained to her that Nixon had been pardoned not by Jimmy Carter, but by Nixon's fellow Republican, Gerald Ford, she was stunned.

One young man, a gas station attendant, proudly informed me

that he was planning to vote for Jesse Jackson. I broke the news to him that Jackson had failed to gain his party's nomination (this was two months after the Democratic convention) and that, as a matter of fact, he hadn't even been a candidate that year.

"Really?" he asked, clearly disappointed. Then he shrugged. "Then I guess I'll vote for Nader."

I did meet two Crook County citizens whose opinions I respected. One middle-aged shopper told me that she made it a point to always vote against the incumbent because the longer a politician holds office, the more corrupt he becomes. Thus she had voted for Jimmy Carter in 1976, Ronald Reagan in 1980, Walter Mondale in 1984, Michael Dukakis in 1988, Bill Clinton in 1992 and Bob Dole in 1996. She was planning to vote for George Bush because he was less of an incumbent than Gore.

A ninety-three-year-old man, whom I met at a senior citizen's luncheon, gave me a succinct synopsis of his electoral history.

"The first time I was eligible to vote was 1928. With great enthusiasm I cast my vote for Herbert Hoover. When I saw how things turned out with him, I never voted again."

After days of discouraging, mostly imbecilic responses, I finally found the interviewee of my dreams: Winston Phelps, the sixty-five-year-old manager of a stationery store. Mr. Phelps, like Crook County itself, had always voted with the winner, in his case going back to the days of Dwight Eisenhower. With bated breath, I waited for Winston Phelps to share with me his choice in the upcoming election.

"George Bush," he announced without hesitation.

"Why?"

Mr. Phelps appeared taken aback by this sudden rough question. I got the distinct impression that he hadn't given it much thought.

"I guess it's because I..." He broke off, his eyes rolling toward a shelf of Scotch tape. "I guess it's because Gore looks like uncooked bread dough and Nader has a dark complexion."

My article was a big hit back in New York. Lute Wisdom summed up its appeal with these unappealingly blunt words: "You gave our readers just what they wanted. They're fascinated by the world outside the City. Rural America is exotic to them. At the same time, you reinforced their need to believe that they are immeasurably superior to the dumb yokels who inhabit the rest of the country." He also told me that the key to my success was my "spunky good looks." He said I was curvaceous enough to get the men to talk; yet I had a non-threatening girl-next-door aura that allowed the women to let down their guards as well.

After the election was over and Crook County voted for Bush, I was sent back out into "Yokelland." This time my assignment, which would ultimately transform my life by earning me my own column, was to investigate an epidemic of cattle mutilations that was plaguing eastern Colorado.

In reviewing the newspaper clippings sent in by a *New York Insider* reader who had received them from his mother in Denver, I learned that a basic pattern linked most of the forty cases which had been reported in the previous two months. The deed was always done at night. There were never any witnesses. No footprints could be found, nor were there any vehicle tracks. There were no signs of struggle. The victimized cow was devoid of blood, yet there were no traces of blood nearby. Several organs were missing, usually the sex organs. The rectum had been cut out cleanly, and sometimes other body parts, such as the tongue or patches of skin, were also gone. The bodies were always described as having been carved up with "surgical precision."

Before leaving New York, I did some library research and discovered that cattle mutilations actually had a long history, dating back to a rash of incidents on the Scotch-English border in 1810. The modern story appeared to begin in November 1963, when cattle near Gallipolis, Ohio, were discovered having been cut up with, you guessed it, "surgical precision." This remained an isolated episode until September 9, 1967, when a gelding named Snippy was found on the Harry King Ranch near Alamosa, Colorado, with blood drained and organs missing. Incidents of cattle mutilations occurred sporadically during the early 1970s, peaked between 1973 and 1976, and had continued at a more modest, though steady rate, ever since. Since the demise of poor Snippy, more than 10,000 cattle mutilations had been reported. They had ranged as far north as Minnesota, as far west as California and as far east and south as Oklahoma, Arkansas and Texas. Now, after twenty-five years, they were back in Colorado.

When I arrived in Colorado, I discovered that the local cattlemen were up in arms. The Elbert County Livestock Association had even offered a cash reward for information leading to the arrest and conviction of anyone responsible for the mutilations. Wild theories were being traded in bars and shopping malls. The lack of tracks and one report of mysterious lights had led to speculation that UFOs were involved.

Bud Pinckney, a multimillionaire rancher whose name had surfaced during the Iran-Contra hearings because of his hefty donations to the Nicaraguan Contras, practically pinned me against a wall and then angrily lectured me about his theory.

"Yes, there are flying objects, but they sure as hell aren't unidentified. They're military helicopters that pick up the cattle, carry them to a secret spot for nerve gas experiments, kill them and then lower the remains to the ground somewhere else."

Archie Norchmann pulled me aside at a cattlemen's meeting and, eyes flitting back and forth in search of eavesdroppers, told me that Bud Pinckney was "full of shit. The true story is that the mutilations are part of a modern-day range war. Pinckney and a few other powerful ranchers are trying to intimidate smaller ranchers, like me, and scare us into selling our land."

While I was in Colorado, a new theory surfaced: the cattle mutilations were the work of devil worshippers who were using the blood and body parts of animals for ghastly predawn rituals. For some reason which I was never able to determine, suspicion fell on the members of the Church of Satan of Greeley, Colorado.

I think my interview with the Church of Satan's minister, the Rev. Bob Klum, was a major factor in turning my article into such a popular piece. Reverend Bob, as he was known, was adamant in defense of the members of his congregation, his "grotto."

"Now that the Communists are on the ropes," he complained, "we Satanists are getting blamed for everything. My mom and dad own cattle themselves. Why would I want to see cattle killed?" The plight of these poor, persecuted devil worshippers surely touched the hearts of my readers back in New York, but without a doubt the highlight of my investigation was my dramatic solution to the mystery of cattle mutilations.

At a bar in Fort Collins, I met Barry Colfax, a charmingly bashful member of the sheriff's department, who also happened to have a gorgeous body. It was Barry's opinion that all this "stuff" about cattle mutilations was "hogwash," mass hysteria. "The whole thing is caused by predators."

"Predators?" I asked. I associated the word with lecherous men at bars in New York City and wasn't sure what he meant.

"Sure. Coyotes, wolves, dog packs, weasels, skunks, buzzards. A cow dies naturally and the predators eat her up before the ranchers notice."

I challenged Barry to prove his theory. Three nights later, with the permission of Barry's boss, he and I and another young sheriff named Buddy Brewster hauled a terminally ill cow out to a remote field. Barry put the suffering cow out of its misery and then the three of us, with adequate provisions of food and drink, settled in behind some bushes to watch the show.

What went on in our cozy little bunker was memorable in itself, but the activity out in the field was more relevant to my story. By midday a hoard of buzzards had discovered the carcass and torn it to shreds, sucking up the blood, feasting on the sex organs and munching on the eyes. After the buzzards had had their fill, the blowflies moved in. Swarms of them cleaned up the rectum and the eyes, creating the appearance of "surgical precision." After thirty-two hours the bovine corpse displayed all the characteristics of a classic mutilation case. Barry postulated that ninety-five percent of cattle mutilations could be attributed to predators and that the other five percent were probably the work of pranksters and copycat killers.

Back in my motel room, I wrote nonstop until the piece was completed. Then I flew home to New York.

My article, "Cattle Mutilations: Solved at Last," was an enormous success. Hiding in their claustrophobic New York flats, *Insider* readers laughed at the gullibility of the Colorado yokels, sneered at the pomposity of Bud Pinckney, chuckled at the anguish of Reverend Bob, and cooed admiringly over my hero, the Noble Savage, Barry Colfax. To my great surprise, "Solved at Last" was the most popular article to appear in the New York *Insider* since "A User's Guide to Manhattan's Prostitutes." Lute Wisdom doubled my salary on the spot and gave me my own column.

At that time I was pursuing a disciplined social life. I stayed home weeknights. On Friday nights I went out with my Columbia friends to a club or to the movies. On Saturday nights I went on dinner dates with my boyfriend, Jerry. I don't want to dwell on my relationship with Jerry because it's long over and I am embarrassed that I spent as much time as I did with such a shallow person. However he did play a role in my search for the flying boy of Calhoun County, Tennessee, so I can't ignore him altogether.

Suffice it to say that, at the time, I was attracted to Jerry because he was intelligent, witty, handsome and self-assured. He was a rising star in the field of political advertising. He was contemptuous of the pea-brained voters who fell prey to the campaign spots that he produced. When I told him about my promotion, he was thrilled.

"I'm envious," he told me. "I have to pretend that I respect the average American; you can be honest and rip him to shreds."

I felt a twinge of discomfort when he said that, but I was so dazzled by my sudden success that I forgot about it quickly. Sensing that I had taken a first big step on the road to fame and fortune, I threw myself into my work.

Reports of a poltergeist in a middle-class home outside of Albany, New York, had attracted a good deal of attention when a local television station had filmed plates falling off shelves and a door slamming open and shut of its own accord. I took the train up north and leaped at the opportunity to use all the techniques I had learned in my university course in Investigative Journalism. Having done a bit of research on poltergeists beforehand, I was not surprised to discover that the family that owned the victimized house included a teenaged girl: an unhappy, sexually frustrated fourteen-year-old. I began my interview with her by appearing sympathetic and even a bit soppy. After listening to her whine about her parents for fifteen minutes, I suddenly bore into her and demanded that she confess that this "poltergeist activity" was really a clever hoax on her part. She instantly burst into tears and then, while I labored to hide my shock, she did confess. She and a girlfriend had burrowed into spaces between the walls and constructed an elaborate system of weights, pulleys and huge magnets.

Lute Wisdom rewarded me for exposing not only the girl's hoax, but the stupidity of the Albany television station. He gave me unlimited travel privileges in pursuit of stories for my column as long as I stayed within the continental United States.

The next morning I flew to eastern Washington state, where an old codger had claimed to have photographed a Sasquatch, a Bigfoot. Fresh from my poltergeist exposé, I expected another hoax. Instead I found a completely sincere seventy-eight-year-old mountain man, friendly, but a bit demented: a classic yokel. His photograph, taken with an ancient Kodak Brownie, showed a furry, man-shaped smudge set against a snow-covered slope. I borrowed the negative and drove it to the University of Washington, where I paid to have a print computer-enhanced. The Sasquatch turned out to be a tree.

For several months I raced around the United States in pursuit of crackpots, suckers, pranksters and con men whose farfetched claims would entertain my readers back in New York. There was the man in Lima, Ohio, who claimed he could turn water into gasoline by adding a mysterious green powder; the Mormon Boy Scout troop that thought they had seen a naked family living in an inaccessible cave in Utah; and the Arkansas widow who was so sure that trolls were invading her vegetable garden that she convinced the local police to set up a video camera in her okra patch.

Once in a while, a copy of my column would find its way to one of the yokels I had written about and I would receive an angry reply in the mail. I had little trouble ignoring most of these indignant responses, but every now and then a poignant note from someone I had falsely befriended would prick my conscience and I would brood about it for days. However, it wasn't until the Angelita Martínez case that I began to feel really uneasy about what I was doing.

Angelita Martínez was a twelve-year-old who had been killed while walking home from school in northwestern Phoenix when a drunk driver lost control of his vehicle, jumped the curb and slammed her against a wall. The following night, her distraught father, Arturo Martínez, visited the spot where the tragedy had taken place, looked up at the vacant billboard directly above the wall that was still specked with his daughter's blood, and saw a shadow in the shape of the Virgin Mary. News of this miracle spread quickly throughout the surrounding neighborhoods, and people poured out of their homes, all of them verifying that, indeed, the Blessed Virgin had appeared, her hands uplifted, palms to the sky, as if to say that poor little Angelita was now safe in Heaven, protected by God.

Each evening at dusk, crowds gathered to await the miracle. By the time I arrived on the fifth night, the normally heavily trafficked thoroughfare was shut down by 8,000 devoted Catholics, not all of them Hispanic. When the skies became dark, they pointed and oohed and aahed. To me the shadow, which was created by a high-intensity security lamp backlighting a barbed-wire fence and some trees, looked as much like a turkey or a peacock as it did the Virgin Mary. You had to be as fanatical as my Grandmother Farrell to perceive on this abandoned, peeling billboard anything remotely spiritual. I chatted with ten or twelve awestruck bystanders, respectfully interviewed Arturo Martínez and took the next flight back to New York.

But when I sat down to write about the gullibility of these religious yokels, my fingers refused to press down on the keys of my computer. I found myself wondering what kind of lives they had stepped out of when they drove over to see that billboard and what sort of hope and solace it provided them. When my Grandfather Watkins died, everyone talked about what a rich, full life he had lived. No one could say that about Angelita Martínez.

I went ahead and wrote the article, mocking the Catholic yokels, so trapped in their narrow-minded pseudo-spirituality that they were able to convince themselves that barbed wire was a message from Heaven. I wrote it, but I didn't feel good about it. When "It's a Bird, It's a Turkey, It's…the Virgin Mary" was printed, I refused to look at it.

CHAPTER 3

CRISIS OF CONSCIENCE

That evening I had a dinner date with Jerry. Before leaving my apartment, I did some hard thinking about my family and how having two parents who were so different had left me with conflicting feelings about people who were odd or out of the mainstream.

To my mother there were only two ways of doing anything: her way and the wrong way. It was inconceivable to her that there existed a second correct method of performing a task besides her own way. It was also beyond the realm of possibility that she might change her mind about anything.

My mother imposed her stubbornness on everyone she knew, but I observed its awful effects primarily in her relations with my brother, Kyle. I can remember when I was five years old, my brother, who was eight, ran into the kitchen, bursting with pride. "Mommy, Mommy, look at the drawing I made of our house." My mother put aside the broom she was using to sweep the floor and studied Kyle's masterpiece. After a few moments of silence, she began picking it apart. The windows were too big. The door was off center. The chimney was the wrong color. The oak tree in front of the house was not realistic; it looked like a lollipop. Kyle sniffed, his eyes watered, then he cried even though he tried hard not to. "Don't be such a baby," said my mother.

Another time she ordered him to wash the dishes after dinner. Kyle attacked the job with enthusiasm, determined to do it perfectly. My mother stood over his shoulder, refraining from comment until he was completely finished. Even the pots and pans sparkled. Not one speck of food remained. My mother could not bring herself to utter a word of praise. Instead she shook her head grimly and announced, "When you clean a pot or pan always use a circular motion instead of scrubbing back and forth. That way you don't scrape the metal."

By the time he was eleven years old, Kyle had given up trying to please our mother. "It can't be done," he explained to me. "If we let her control us, we'll stop being ourselves and end up being extensions of her." I had to ask my father what "extension" meant, but I got the message.

After that, Kyle and my mother were constantly at war. Then, when he was thirteen, she caught him masturbating. She called him so many names that I had to cover my ears even though I was two rooms away. She told him he was "damned for eternity," and that there was no hope for him to redeem himself ever.

"At least I used a circular motion," he smugly countered. But a couple of weeks later Kyle suffered the first of his nervous breakdowns.

He was sitting across from me at the breakfast table. I was munching my cornflakes and milk, a ten-year-old trying to sneak a look at the newspaper comic strips while my mother was busy in another room.

"Everything needs to be in order," said my brother suddenly. "These cornflakes are dirty."

I looked up, thinking he was being droll. But his eyes were glazed, the corners of his mouth twisted. "Mars, to the right, Venus, a bit to the left." After that he was so lost that all he did was babble. When my mother returned, she thought he was faking, putting on an act to avoid going to school. I tried to convince her that something was wrong, but she wouldn't listen. She yelled at Kyle and ordered him to get his books and get going. He giggled at something I couldn't see. I ran and got my Dad, who was shaving. Back in the kitchen my mother was six inches from Kyle, screaming into his ear, "You're a bum; your life is wasted!"

My father shoved her aside, studied Kyle for a few seconds, and called the paramedics. Everyone assumed he was on drugs. When the blood tests came back negative, the diagnosis switched to psychotic break. I assumed that my mother would be consumed by guilt, since it was obviously her fault. But, oh no, not Mom. As far as she was concerned, Kyle had brought it on himself with his stubbornness, and my father had contributed with his antireligious intellectualism, his psychological theories causing Kyle to be spoiled.

Until then I had done my best to cooperate with my mother, if only to avoid the sort of attacks she had launched against my brother. Now I began to hate her.

Before long, Kyle entered a regular cycle: psychotic break, institutionalization, recovery, several months of normality at home, and then another psychotic break. Each time it became clear that Kyle had to be sent to the mental hospital, my mother would pack a suitcase of clothes for him, actually whistling as she worked, a smile on her face, as if his mental illness were proof that my father's theories were poppycock and that she had been right all along.

My mother was such a loathsome person that it's convenient to assume that my father was a saint. In fact, he responded to my mother's attempts to control him by withdrawing from the family and immersing himself in the demands of his profession. This worked well for him, but for Kyle and me it was like being raised in a one-parent family. As a professor of psychology, he could have done so much. He could have at least protected us. Instead, he failed us by abdicating his parental responsibilities.

I will say this, though, for my father, in the midst of all the troubles in my family, he accepted a one-year fellowship at UCLA. My brother had already been institutionalized twice by this time, and my father thought the temporary change of scenery might do him some good.

So, when I was thirteen years old, we left Timberlake, where half the boys were named Junior, and moved to Los Angeles, metropolitan population: nine million. I was thrown into a public school on the affluent west side of town. Just like in the movies, the students of Paul Revere Junior High School confronted gangs, drugs and early loss of virginity. I was in shock for several weeks. Fortunately, I had already developed the "spunky good looks" that serve me so well as a journalist. My hardest problem socially was choosing which clique to join. All the kids were so bored with each other that they all wanted me.

I settled in with an intellectual group, but I still felt like an outsider. I found myself fascinated, haunted really, by the school's outcasts. The student body at Paul Revere was so large and so diverse that there seemed to be a clique for everyone. Black lesbians, Jewish bridge addicts, neo-Nazis with pierced ears. If you looked carefully you could find a soul mate no matter how esoteric your interests.

And yet there were an unfortunate few who were so strange that they slipped through the cracks. For some reason, the city of Los Angeles promoted a policy of mainstreaming the mentally ill. I developed a morbid fascination with these sad cases. There were three students in particular whom I observed and eventually tried to befriend. Perhaps because of the problems of my own brother, the three I chose were all white males.

The first was Percival Smith. How thoughtless his parents must have been to brand him with such a name. Percival was still in the eighth grade even though he was sixteen years old. He had the maturity of a four-year-old. He was obsessed with vomit. With his crew-cut and thick glasses, he would jab his finger at you, cry out, "You vomit!" and then cackle wildly as if he had just cut you to shreds with the cleverest put down in history. Percival had an unusual hobby: he memorized the date on which each of his classmates had most recently vomited. If you missed a day or two of school because of illness, Percival would anxiously approach you upon your return. "Did you vomit?" he would ask. If the answer was "yes," he would walk away gravely. Six months later, he would come up to you in the cafeteria and say loudly, "You vomit: October 14, 1991." He might repeat this once or twice. Then he would cackle and walk away.

Those boys who enjoyed picking on weak classmates had a field day with Percival. They would pretend to be his friend, then flip his books, point their fingers at him and imitate his cackle. The cruelest boys would pretend to have vomited when they really hadn't, thus fouling Percival's mental filing system with false data. When Percival realized that he was being made fun of, he would fly into a tearful rage that tore at my heart. I wanted to help him, to hug him, but the best I could do was to listen attentively to the catalogue of his own vomits. Those recitations were the only times he seemed at peace: "February 6, 1981; December 23, 1982; March 2, 1983…"

Walter Chesbro was the epitome of self-pity. Like Percival, he seemed to be much older than the rest of us. He was big, pale, with kinky, dirty blond hair. He slouched down the hallways, dragging a wool sweater, no matter how hot it was. He talked to no one but himself. At lunch time he would sit alone on a bench, his shoulders hunched forward, shutting out the world. He was the only kid in the school who was exempt from gym class: he was unable—or unwilling—to dress himself. Walter Chesbro was so strange that even the bullies stayed away from him. He was too spooky. One day I caused a sensation at lunch by sitting down beside him. All I could think to say to him was, "Are you all right?" At first he didn't respond. Then he slowly raised his head and looked me right in the eyes. His expression was so woeful and hopeless that I began to cry. After a few seconds, he dropped his gaze and never looked at me again.

The last of my threesome was not mentally disturbed at all, not yet anyway. His name was Patrick McGuinn...*the* Patrick McGuinn. A television star from the age of six, he had his own show by the time he was ten. Comedy fans as far afield as Iceland and Malaysia are still enjoying reruns of his freckled face and curly red hair. In 1991, Patrick's parents decided that he had been too sheltered, that he needed exposure to a normal childhood before it was too late. So they enrolled him at Paul Revere. But it was already too late. The bullies threw pennies at him and called him names. "Asshole." "Show off." "Snob." "Think you're so great." In reality, he didn't appear to be any of these things. But a few weeks of being bombarded with coins and verbal abuse forced him to put up a thick protective shell. He became the haughty stereotype they wanted him to be. Patrick was hostile to my early approaches, but toward the end of what was to be the only year at Paul Revere for both of us, he finally relaxed in my presence.

Just a few days before this present moral crisis of mine, I picked up the *Times* and discovered Patrick's obituary. He had committed suicide. The obit, although concentrating on his inability to cope with life after child stardom, actually mentioned the traumatic effect of his one year in public school. I was startled and shaken to see this in print. I took Patrick's suicide as a personal failure on my part.

I knew that Jerry was uncomfortable with conversations

that dealt with weakness, doubt or uncertainty, but I had no one else to talk with. So that evening, fortified by several glasses of Châteauneuf du Pape at a trendy French restaurant on the Upper West Side, I took a stab at confession.

"I've always considered myself a compassionate human being," I began. "Now, here I am making my living publicly humiliating everyday people who would never dream of treating me as badly as I treat them. I'm stooping to the level of Sean Hannity or Werner Herzog.

Jerry squirmed. "I like Sean Hannity," he said.

Desperate, I tried another angle. "Jerry, I'm afraid that I'm becoming like my mother."

Jerry shrugged his shoulders.

I told him about the middle school year when I had reached out to Percival Smith and Walter Chesbro. I told him that I felt guilty about Patrick McGuinn's suicide.

"But, Suzy, surely you realize that you couldn't be expected at the age of thirteen or fourteen to say just the right words to counter a lifetime of unhappiness."

"I know, but don't you see, since that time I've transformed myself from someone who was friendly to outcasts into someone who mocks and exploits similarly harmless people?"

"But it's part of your job."

"Maybe I should change my job."

I mentioned that Jerry felt uncomfortable with moral ambiguity. He responded to my crisis of conscience by trying to change the subject.

But I persisted. "Jerry, I said," you do see why I'm afraid of becoming like my mother, don't you? In fact, I'm even worse. She says mean things about people behind their backs because she hates everyone. I don't hate anyone, yet I say mean things about people anyway, and I even do it in public. I've got to do something to change myself and I've got to do it fast. You do understand, don't you?"

I don't think that Jerry did understand. Or, if he did, he didn't care. Fortunately, at the same time that I was experiencing my crisis of conscience, I stumbled upon a bimonthly magazine from London called *Fortean Times*. Subtitled "The Journal of Strange Phenomena," its pages were devoted entirely to the same sort of offbeat events that I was writing about. Through this periodical I learned of other, similar publications. In retrospect, it seems incredible that I had been preparing my column for so long without knowing that this network of like-minded people existed.

The *Fortean Times* and its cousin publications were dedicated to the memory of Charles Fort (1874-1932), a New Yorker who spent much of his adult life pouring through scientific journals in search of anomalies—facts and incidents which, inconveniently, could not to be explained by commonly accepted theories. He called these bits of information "the damned" because scientists, acting like religious dogmatists, had excommunicated them. In his lifetime, Fort was wrongly accused of being "the arch enemy of science." In fact, he respected the scientific method. What irked him was arrogant scientists who ignored the basic rules of objective scientific inquiry and instead tried to match the facts to theories they had already decided were irrefutable.

I worried that longtime serious students of strange events, such as the editors of the *Fortean Times*, would be hostile to a newcomer like me who wrote for a circulation ten times their own. Fortunately, the opposite was true: they were delighted that someone out there had a big enough budget to follow through on some of the leads they had collected.

Reading the *Fortean Times* I saw a way out of my dilemma. What if, like Charles Fort, decades earlier, I chose as the target of my cynical attacks not everyday credulous people, but pompous, know-it-all "experts?" That way I could salve my conscience and still maintain the mocking tone that readers of the *New York Insider* expected and loved.

My first opportunity to try this new strategy came when the Associated Press distributed a brief filler about the sudden fall from the sky of several hundred small frogs that landed in a schoolyard in Shreveport, Louisiana. Like most people, I had been trained to believe that strange objects simply do not fall from the sky, that such events only take place in fairy tales like Chicken Little and Henny Penny.

And yet, unexpected objects do come flying down at us from time to time. On September 6, 1962, for example, a 21-pound piece of a Soviet satellite, Sputnik IV, crashed into an intersection in Manitowoc, Wisconsin. On March 8, 1976, a 3,902-pound stony meteorite smashed to earth in the Haupi Commune near the Chinese city of Kirin. On Monday morning, September 25, 1978, Mary C. Farrell was sitting in her parked car with her eight-month-old son, when a human body crashed through the windshield. The body had been thrown from a jet that had been hit by a small plane. The descent of space junk, meteorites and plane crash victims are easily explained. But what about tiny frogs? I knew from my mother that the second plague on Egypt in the Bible included frogs from the sky, but I couldn't imagine what Shreveport had done wrong to be singled out by God for such slimy punishment.

Fortunately, the Shreveport Frog Fall, which lasted for fifteen minutes, occurred while hundreds of children, aged six to eleven were outside. In fact, several of the children had to fish the little critters out of their hair. Still at the age where the world is basically magic anyway, these kids took the frog fall in stride. Some of them held a contest to see how many they could stomp to death. The more pacific of the children took the tiny frogs in their hands and studied them. I spoke with six different teachers who witnessed the event. The teachers, who were thrilled by this break in their routine, took me to their classrooms and showed me dozens of the frogs, which they had kept alive in hastily assembled "frogariums."

"How did you explain the phenomenon to your students?" I asked the assembled teachers. Then the excitement began. Men and women who spend six hours a day posing as the voice of authority to innocent little children have a tendency to lecture everyone they know, even adults. And they don't like to be interrupted.

"Whirlwind," pronounced teacher Buford Harris, a middle-aged white man with a neat salt-and-pepper beard. "In the middle of a storm, a whirlwind or waterspout sucks up the frogs out of a pond or stream, whisks them away and drops them elsewhere."

"I doubt it," countered Alice Davis, a young black teacher. Her tone told me that they had been having this argument ever since the frogs had fallen three days earlier. "In the first place, there was no storm that day. The sky was clear and there was only the slightest of breezes. Besides, how could a whirlwind be so selective? When the frogs fell, there was nothing with them: no fish, no plants, no mud, and no water for that matter. Not even a pebble."

"So, what's your explanation," I asked.

"Birds."

"Birds?"

"A flock of high-flying birds, having eaten the frogs, flew away, then decided it wasn't such a treat after all and threw them up."

I thought of Percival Smith. What a paradise this school would have been for him. Even the birds vomit.

"It would take dozens of birds to have scooped up so many frogs," countered Buford Harris. "Why would so many birds disgorge at once?"

"Maybe birds are like sheep," offered Alice Davis. "Whatever the leader does, all the others follow."

Willard Gompf, a tall young white man, shook his head cynically. "I put my money on a different answer: practical jokers. Someone with nothing better to do collected the frogs, took off in a small plane and dumped them on us."

Lute Wisdom enjoyed my article on the Shreveport Frog Fall, which I concluded with a favorite quote from Charles Fort, himself. Commenting on a case in which two species of perch appeared in a newly dug-ditch after a week of rain, Fort wrote, "The sending of fresh water fishes to a salt-water lake is no more out of place than, for instance, is the sending of chaplains to battleships." Because I lampooned the teachers and their theories, Lute failed to notice the subtle change in my perspective.

Emboldened, I pursued my anti-expert attack on a more controversial topic. My brother Kyle, with a little extra free time on his hands now that his son had entered pre-school, had taken up a new hobby: collecting newspaper accounts of murders. Each morning he visited the library at Wake Forest University and read through twenty papers, looking for the "best" of the forty-five or so murders that were committed each day in the United States. I asked him if he might, while he was at it, look out for any strange deaths.

One day, a letter arrived from Kyle containing a photocopy of an article from the *St. Petersburg, Florida Times*. It was an account, complete with surprisingly gruesome details, of the bizarre death of Robert Barbaroma, a sixty-seven-year-old retired welder. Neighbors on the third floor of Mr. Barbaroma's apartment noticed smoke coming out from underneath his door. They called the superintendent, who opened the door. The neighbors and the superintendent followed the smoke to its source, a smoldering pile of ashes about four feet from Mr. Barbaroma's bed. Next to the pile was all that remained of their friend: his left foot, still encased in its leather slipper. Sifting through the ashes, police investigators also found a piece of spine, a shrunken skull and a liver, extra well-done. What made the case strange was that the fire that had consumed Mr. Barbaroma had barely touched anything else. The wall, two feet away, was sooty, but not scorched, while a pile of newspapers ready for recycling, less than a foot away, was not burned at all.

Following the trail of burn marks, the police concluded that Robert Barbaroma had fallen asleep while smoking. Awakening to discover himself on fire, he had run to the bathroom, thrown his nightclothes in the tub, poured water on himself with a drinking glass and returned to the bedroom where he collapsed and eventually turned to ash. Although no mention was made of it in the article, I recognized Mr. Barbaroma's death as a classic example of a most unusual phenomenon: spontaneous human combustion. SHC, as it is known among Forteans, describes cases in which a living human being is consumed by fire and reduced to ashes despite the lack of serious damage to the surrounding area.

By the time I got down to St. Petersburg, the Barbaroma case, while not actually becoming a *cause célèbre*, was attracting some local interest. Police attempts to close what appeared to be a sticky case were thwarted by Mr. Barbaroma's numerous friends. An inquest was held. A professional cremator testified that the only way to shrink a skull and to turn human bones to ash was to burn it for one and a half hours at 1,700 degrees Fahrenheit. Further testimony revealed that Mr. Barbaroma was a militant nonsmoker.

The St. Petersburg police department, responding to community pressure, agreed to re-open the case. They refused to consider spontaneous combustion as a possible explanation and instead concluded that Robert Barbaroma had been murdered away from his home, his body cremated and the remains returned to his room. The police chief, inspired by a letter to the editor of the *St. Petersburg Times*, suggested that the murderer had read the novel *Bleak House*, wherein the author, none other than Charles Dickens, describes the death by spontaneous combustion of the fictional rag-and-bottle seller, Krook. In other words, while refusing to acknowledge the existence of spontaneous human combustion, the police were willing to dub this a case of fake spontaneous combustion!

Back in New York, I got on the phone and contacted as many "experts" as I could, mostly highly respected pathologists. Several of them listened to my summary of the physical details, concluded that I had my facts wrong and hung up. Those who were willing to consider the possibility of SHC came up with an amazing variety of definitive explanations. Dr. Max Ronningen of Johns Hopkins suggested that Robert Barbaroma was one of the one in one hundred thousand people who can build up a charge of up to 30,000 volts, and that static electricity had ignited him. He had no explanation as to why the fire was so localized. Dr. Alfred Boas of the University of California-Berkeley, fell back on the classic nineteenth century theory that victims of spontaneous combustion were alcoholics who had saturated their insides with flammable spirits.

"But all of his friends say Barbaroma never drank alcohol," I explained.

"He probably did it secretly," replied the expert.

Dr. Penelope Costain of the Mayo Clinic had once appeared in a BBC-TV report debunking spontaneous human combustion. When I told her the facts of the Barbaroma case, she was contemptuous. With barely concealed impatience she described to me "human candle syndrome." Typically, an obese person, usually drunk or otherwise dulled, falls asleep in bed or in a stuffed chair. A dropped cigarette or a spark from a fireplace ignites the bedding or the upholstery, which serves as the wick in the "human candle." The body fat serves as the wax. Slowly but surely the body burns, smoldering rather than bursting into flames that would cause the fire to spread.

I was impressed by Dr. Costain's explanation—except that Robert Barbaroma was not obese, but lean and muscular, and he had been alert enough to try to save himself by discarding his "wick"—his nightclothes. Like my mother and my grandmother, Dr. Costain did not like to be challenged or contradicted.

"I'm sure that the victim was fatter than you think. Undoubtedly his friends have described him incorrectly because, consciously or unconsciously, they prefer the romance of a mysterious death to the reality of a more prosaic one."

There you have it—Expert's syndrome: if the facts don't fit the theory, refuse to accept the facts.

"Spontaneous Human Combustion: A Burning Controversy" was so well received by readers of the *Insider* that Lute Wisdom was forced to give me another raise. By this time I was being paid so well that my crisis of conscience vanished for many months. But it did come back. Lute became annoyed with my persistent mocking of experts, so I was forced to engage in periodic yokel-bashing in order to vary the tone of my column. My old guilt returned.

My emotional state was complicated by the fact that my boyfriend Jerry was completely unsympathetic. Whenever I tried to share with him my turmoil, he dismissed it as "feminine weakness," and changed the subject to politics. The situation came to a head one Sunday morning as we sipped coffee in his living room.

"When I started writing my column," I began, "I approached each investigation with the goal of exposing hoaxes and/or soft thinking. But now when I go out into Yokelland I find myself wishing that the strange objects flying over Hardin, Montana, really are visitors from outer space or that the midday darkening of the sky in Fisher, Pennsylvania, really is caused by forces beyond our comprehension. I guess I want to go back to those early years of my childhood when everything from butterflies to electricity seemed to be created by magic."

Jerry was clearly irritated with me. "You're like a hostage who takes the side of his kidnappers," he said. "I thought you were sharper than that."

I jumped up, gathered my things and left his apartment, never to return.

CHAPTER 4

THE LETTER

Nostalgic, disillusioned, unfulfilled, I was unusually receptive when, the very next day, I discovered on my desk a letter postmarked Mosquito Lick, Kentucky.

I should note that by this time I was receiving quite a bit of fan mail. Many of my readers sent me clippings from their local newspapers and some of these clippings proved to be useful leads for my column. I also received numerous handwritten letters that never, ever, proved useful. They were always sent by semiliterate yokels who had seen UFOs or by complete fruitcakes who claimed to be in contact with psychic forces from the Inner Earth. Still, feeling a sense of obligation to my loyal readers, I was compelled to read every one of these pathetic messages.

Attracted by the unusual postmark on the letter before me, and wondering how someone in Mosquito Lick, Kentucky, could even find a copy of the *New York Insider*, I tore open the envelope and pulled out three sheets of folded blue paper. Before I had even read a word I could tell that this letter was different from the others. The handwriting was exquisitely neat, the letters well-formed and clear, without any affectations or curlicues. I reproduce the contents in their entirety:

Dear Suzy Watkins,

I am sure you are a very busy person and I hate to take up your time, but I think you may want to follow up a story I know about.

I am a schoolteacher in a small town in south-central Kentucky. I have to admit that it is pretty backward here, but I try to keep up with the outside world by subscribing to the *New York Insider* and other publications.

My mother, Violet Poltrain, recently deceased, served as midwife in Bethel and neighboring counties for fifty-two years. Doctors and hospitals have always been viewed in this part of the country with great suspicion. They are also considered too costly, so my mother always had her hands full with work (so to speak).

Twenty years ago, in August 1988, my mother came home late at night from a delivery. I was seventeen years old at the time. I adored my mother. Whenever she went out on a delivery, I would stay up and wait for her. When she returned, I would make her a cup of hot chocolate and she would tell me the details of the delivery. These late nights shared with my mother were so special that I wouldn't miss a one even if I had school the next morning and I had to do without sleep. Even if the night's story was a sad one, a stillbirth, my mother would share with me all that had happened.

But this one night, the one in August 1988, was different. My mother came home shaken. There was fear and terror in her eyes. When I asked her what had happened, she shook her head and refused to answer. She even refused to drink her hot chocolate. For the next few days she went around the house in an agitated state. I would say she was spooked.

Five days later she was called out for another delivery. This time she came back in her usual good spirits and our lives picked up as before. During thirty-two years of midwifery, from the time I was five years old until she died, this one spooky birth was the only one she didn't tell me about.

I was haunted by the mystery of the incident, but I held my tongue and never asked my mother about it. Two weeks ago, my mother died at the age of seventy-seven. As her strength began to fade, I started to worry that I would never learn the secret of that night in 1988. I could see that there weren't many words left in her. I knew I should have let her use her remaining energy more appropriately, but instead I pleaded with her to satisfy my curiosity. She was reluctant, but she loved me and did it anyway.

Here is what she told me: the pregnant woman and her husband, both of them teenagers, had only arrived in the county a week earlier. They were renting a shed from Hawley Huskins, an eccentric recluse who lived in the woods about fifteen miles outside of Mosquito Lick. The couple told my mother their names were Tom and Tammy, although my mother suspected these weren't their real names. The couple appeared very nervous, as if they were troubled by something deeper than the normal worries of a first birth.

The labor was not unusual; the baby, a boy of about seven pounds, popped out easily.

"He's just fine," said my mother after cleaning him and examining him. The couple was so relieved, my mother feared they might collapse. My mother cut the umbilical cord and started to lift the baby up to show the mother when the baby literally flew out of her hands. He circled the room about halfway and then floated to the dirt floor and began to cry.

My mother and the couple were too shocked to move. The baby flew up again. This time my mother grabbed him and wrapped him in a cloth. She placed him on the mother's breast and he suckled peacefully and fell asleep. Neither my mother nor the couple said anything. My mother tended to "Tammy" and then started to pack her bag. But before she was finished, the baby stirred and took off into the air again, cloth wrapping and all.

The father retrieved the baby and exchanged a terrified look with his wife. My mother was afraid they would kill the baby as soon as she left, so she offered them a deal: if they would promise to raise the baby lovingly and promise not to harm him, my mother would promise not to tell a soul about what she had seen. The couple agreed and the three of them knelt down in prayer, while the father clutched the baby tightly. "Tom" stood at the door to the shack and watched my mother walk to her car. He waved good-bye—and the baby flew out of his arms, bumping his tummy on the door frame. "Tom" frantically snatched hold of him, pulled him inside and slammed shut the door.

The next day, my mother drove out to Hawley Huskins' place to check on the baby and his parents. They were gone. Hawley said they must have cleared out almost immediately because he got up in the middle of the night to use the outhouse and their car was already gone.

That's my story. I can only add that my mother was an extremely sober, levelheaded woman. If she said it happened, it happened.

You can ask anyone: Violet Poltrain never lied, never misled, never even exaggerated. If you want more information I would be glad to help you in any way I can

Sincerely yours,

Helen Poltrain

Ms. Poltrain's letter thrilled me. I wanted desperately to believe that somewhere in the world was a twenty-year-old boy who could fly. I imagined him shy and handsome, secretly harboring his special talent like Clark Kent. I would be his Lois Lane and he would take me in his arms and together we would fly, high above the real world and all its harshness. We would exist instead in a world of daily miracles, just like when I was a child. It would be something like Never-Never Land, except my savior would be muscular Superman rather than fairy-like Peter Pan. And the letter had such a tantalizing air of authenticity!

Now it so happens that I already had some experience with people who claimed they could fly. My biggest article of 2003 had been a report on the Yogic Flying Competition put on by the Transcendental Meditation (TM) organization. This mixture of con men and true believers, followers of the otherwise blameless Maharishi Mahesh Yogi, claimed that they could levitate and even propel themselves through the air. Once a year, the winners of regional contests gathered in Fairfield, Iowa, to compete in the levitation high jump and long jump, a sprint, a hurdles race and a longer race. It sounded great, but in practice it was ridiculous. All the events were held on spongy mattresses, allowing the participants to bounce quite easily. There was not one person who came close to levitating. If Kobe Bryant had practiced for one hour, he would have won every event. In addition to this foolishness, members of the audience had to endure a windy lecture by a short, pasty TM-MD from Southern California, who explained in scientific terms how it was possible to levitate, even though no one actually had.

I was disgusted by their false claims and viciously attacked TM's phoniness in my *Insider* article "Grounded at the Levitation Olympics."

As a teenager in North Carolina I had read the works of Carlos Castaneda, who claimed to have witnessed two Mexican Indian sorcerers, Don Genaro and Don Juan, float and fly. Even then I didn't take his claims as gospel truth, but as metaphors for the spiritual lessons he was trying to teach.

In preparation for my article about the Levitation Olympics, I also did considerable reading on the history of levitation claims. Among the many self-styled mediums who were alleged to have defied gravity were Daniel Dunglas Home, who floated around a drawing room for five minutes; Willy Schneider, who rose to the ceiling, hovered for five minutes and came back down; M. Stainton Moses, an Oxford professor; Juan de Jesus of the Canary Islands; and Carlo Mirabelli, a Brazilian faith healer. None of the accounts of their exploits struck me as credible.

But there was one levitator whose story intrigued me and, even before I received the letter from Helen Poltrain, gave me hope that the inexplicable is possible. He was The Flying Friar, St. Joseph of Cupertino.

Born Giuseppe Desa in the heel of Italy in 1603, the future saint was accepted as a lay brother to the Capuchin order. He worked in the kitchen, but tended to lose himself in ecstatic trances and drop the crockery. He was asked to leave after eight months, but was taken into another order and was accepted into the priesthood in 1628, assuming the name Friar Joseph Maria. He led a life of extreme asceticism, whipping himself, wearing an iron chain around his hips, walking barefoot at all times and following a breadless vegetarian diet. Not satisfied with normal self-flagellation, Joseph spiked his whip with pins and shards of metal. After examining Joseph's blood-spattered cell, his superiors confiscated the spiked whip.

Meanwhile, his shrieks of ecstasy became so loud that they disturbed services. Joseph was sent to Naples to be examined by the Holy Office. While attending mass at the Church of St. Gregory of Armenia in Naples, Joseph suddenly rose into the air with a shriek. According to several nuns of St. Ligorio, who were praying a few feet away, Joseph floated forward, his arms outstretched, and landed on the altar in the midst of flowers and burning candles. The nuns screamed out, "He'll catch fire," but, with another shriek,

Joseph rose again and flew back to where he had originally been kneeling.

Joseph continued to make periodic flights with surprising regularity until his death in 1663. Among the more celebrated witnesses to his airborne activities were Pope Urban VIII and Johann Friedrich, Duke of Brunswick, who was the patron of the German philosopher Gottfried Leibniz. The duke, who observed Joseph's levitations on two occasions in February 1651, was so impressed that he immediately converted from Lutheranism to Catholicism.

Joseph was even known to carry others into the air (these accounts feeding my Lois Lane fantasies). Once, he cured a madman by grabbing the man's hair and levitating with him for fifteen minutes. Witnesses to this particular incident had to be revived with smelling salts.

It is easy to dismiss as fantasy anything out of the ordinary that happened more than 350 years ago, yet the story of St. Joseph of Cupertino contained elements that distinguished it from the other claims of levitation. Most notable were the respectable witnesses, the repeated manifestations and his lack of interest in self-promotion.

The memory of St. Joseph's story was enough to convince me that the letter from Helen Poltrain was worth pursuing. I made immediate plans to fly to Nashville, Tennessee, the closest big city to Mosquito Lick, Kentucky.

When I first began traveling around the United States to research "The Fringe of Reality," I would take whichever car the rental companies offered me. I quickly learned that this was a bad idea: out in Yokelland, you won't be trusted if you drive up in a Toyota or a Saab. So when I arrived at Nashville airport, having already arranged a meeting with Helen Poltrain, I rented a white Chevy Malibu, a nice, bland, unassuming American car.

It's 116 miles from Nashville to Mosquito Lick, Kentucky, but I had plenty of time before my appointment, so, after heading north out of the city, I turned northeast and settled into a leisurely drive up to the Kentucky border. Each town I passed through seemed filled with bleach blondes in shorts. Every station on the radio played country music. I particularly liked "If Heaven Is Like New York City, I'd Rather Go to Hell" and "Sing, Sing Jeffrey Dahmer" with its immortal lyrics: "Jeffrey I don't like your friends/That's all right Ma, just eat your vegetables."

The views of old Hickory Lake and the rolling hills of northern Tennessee were pleasant, but my mind was elsewhere. Helen Poltrain sounded flustered when I had called. At first I wondered if I had made a mistake in pursuing this story. I was afraid that my need to believe in a miracle had blinded me from realizing that she was as loony as the other readers who sent me handwritten letters. But driving along it hit me that Helen Poltrain was one of the few people in Yokelland who read my column. Her nervousness on the phone was easily explained as the reaction of a fan to an admired celebrity. Me, a celebrity: I liked the idea. I liked it so much that I drifted off into a daydream.

I imagined myself discovering a real-life, modern-day version of St. Joseph of Cupertino, a bashful yokel who had kept his talent hidden. I would expose his existence in a brilliant, touching article that would win me international acclaim. Meanwhile, I would bring this culturally sheltered hunk to New York, show him the real world and share with him a passionate romance.

I snapped to when I passed a sign that read "WELCOME TO KENTUCKY, The Bluegrass State." The sign was riddled with bullet holes. Soon the scenery turned too beautiful to ignore. After driving alongside West Pond River Lake, I came upon a white-haired old man in overalls standing beside a stalled Ford pick-up. I slowed down and he waved me to a halt.

"Going up to Aberdeen?" he asked.

"Sure am."

"Can you stop by the Shell station and tell them Will McConnell is stuck on the old Beech Springs highway?"

"Sure thing."

Aberdeen, eight twisting miles up the road, was a thriving metropolis of almost thirteen thousand people. Yet I had no trouble finding the Shell station. Inside the office, a grizzly, overweight man wearing a hunting cap and hunting jacket sat on a stool cleaning his fingernails with a knife. Beside him was a black-bearded man in his thirties.

"Will McConnell's stuck out on the old Beech Springs Highway," I said cheerily.

The two men stared at me without saying a word.

"He needs help," I added, a bit flustered.

"Will McConnell?" said the younger man. "Stuck on the old Beech Springs Highway?"

"Yup."

"I'll go get him."

"By the way," I said, as he slowly gathered his keys, "What's the best route to Mosquito Lick?"

"Mosquito Lick?" The older man was incredulous. "Are you dumb?" Normally I would shrug off this kind of yokel insult because you never know when you'll need to be on good terms with a possible informant. But in this case, I was never going to see him again.

"Yeah, that's me. I must be dumb because I don't know the best route to a town fifty-three miles away, a town so small it doesn't even appear on the Rand McNally state road map for Kentucky. How could I possibly be so stupid?"

The beard and the hunter stared at me, open-mouthed. After a few seconds, the beard spoke up. "You head out the road to Cherryville, turn left where the old mill used to be and go a few more miles. When the road ends, go right at the water tower. After the third stream, take the right fork and after a couple miles that'll lead you right into the backside of Mosquito Lick."

"Thanks."

The older man shook his head sadly, still amazed by the ignorance of today's youth. As soon as I was back in my car I checked the map and plotted my own route. One and a half hours later I was in Mosquito Lick, a main street with four residential cross streets. Helen Poltrain lived on the last of these four, a right turn in front of the Dryfork Diner.

There were only six houses on the block, three on each side. Hers was the middle one on the left. Two stories, freshly painted white, steps leading to a front porch, screened doors and windows. Helen Poltrain appeared in the doorway before I had even closed my car door. At first glance she was surprisingly attractive. She had a slim, well-kept figure. Her knee-length cotton dress was as stylish as a schoolteacher in rural Kentucky could get away with. As I drew closer, bearing my usual sympathetic journalist's smile, I experienced a rush of genuine sympathy for Helen Poltrain. I could see wrinkles forming, the first gray hair, the lonely, frightened eyes. She was a woman who was genetically programmed to turn into a gaunt spinster, a character out of James Agee. But she was fighting it. She didn't wear make-up, but everything else about her—her bright dress, her bouncy hair, her proud stance—was designed to project modernity and worldliness. At this point she was winning the fight.

With a deep breath, Helen Poltrain overcame her nervousness at meeting a celebrity (me, in case you've forgotten), and greeted me warmly with a firm handshake. She spoke to me too, but I responded mechanically because I was overcome by a relapse of my crisis of conscience. During my forays into Yokelland I had concluded that for my purposes there were three categories of people: Objects of Derision, Sympathetic Foils and Sources of Information. Helen Poltrain fell into the third category. I caught myself slipping into my investigative personality, automatically sizing up my target, calculating how to draw out from her the information I wanted so that I could leave as quickly as possible.

Instead, I forced myself to loosen up. I determined that I would let her set the pace for my visit, that I would leave New York behind and be country-friendly, just like people were during my childhood in North Carolina.

Helen Poltrain led me into her living room. Despite the sunlight streaming in through the windows, the room was dark and cold. I imagined that the furnishings—mahogany tables, stuffed chairs and throw rugs oozing decades of comfortable use—were memorials to her deceased mother. The bright Helen Poltrain who subscribed to the *New York Insider* was not willing to give up the objects that evoked her beloved mother. Helen offered, and then served me, tea and biscuits, store-bought, but very un-Kentucky.

"I know you're a very busy person," she began, "so..."

"Oh, no, no," I interrupted. "My job isn't as hectic as you might think," I lied. "Still, I envy you living in such a beautiful area. I'm sure you must be overwhelmed by work yourself, but sometimes I think I'd prefer the life of a country schoolteacher to the chaos of the big city." Then I told her about my childhood in Timberlake, North Carolina, and my own desire to get out.

Helen Poltrain laughed lightly. "Do you remember the English children's story about the country mouse and the city mouse? City mouse visits his cousin in the country, but he can't stand the simple food, the quiet, the fear of huge animals like horses and cows. So he takes Country Mouse to the city, but Country Mouse is frightened by the cars and the cats and can't stand eating table scraps. In the end, Country Mouse is content in the country and City Mouse is content in the city.

"My mother used to tell me a different tale. Even though she never left southern Kentucky, she used to tell me the story of 'The Fancy Plate and the Everyday Plate.' It seems that there were two shelves in the kitchen, one for the fancy dishes that were used only on special occasions and one for the everyday dishes that were used for breakfast, lunch and dinner. This one fancy plate, all delicate with curlicue designs, used to stare out of a crack in the shelf door and watch the everyday plates. Each morning they'd be hauled down, covered with food and placed before a child who would wolf down his meal with pleasure. Then they'd be washed with soap and warm water and set on a rack to dry in the sun. Same thing at lunch and dinner. The fancy plate was so envious that one night she crawled out of her shelf, scuttled across the kitchen counter and climbed into the shelf with the everyday dishes.

"'Oh, if only I could be like you,' she told the top dish, always out and about, seeing the world, being appreciated by the children. Hard work, warm baths, sitting in the sun. I wish that I could be an everyday plate.'

"'Ha! It's not as great a life as it seems. We're always being banged around and chipped. Every time they wash us, we get battered and bruised. No sooner are we dry than it's time to go back to work. And the children, they never even notice us. No, I'd rather be a fancy plate. You get to rest for months at a time. And when you do get used, you're handled ever so carefully, everyone praises how you look and when they wash you, they're so careful!'

"'I've got an idea,' says the fancy plate. 'Why don't we switch places?'

"So the fancy plate covered the chips on the everyday plate with her curlicues and the everyday plate knocked a few pieces off the fancy plate. The fancy plate got on top of the stack of everyday dishes and the everyday plate scampered across the kitchen and climbed in with the fancy dishes. The next day, the fancy plate got to work all day long, while the old everyday plate got her first real rest in years. And they both lived happily ever after."

I chuckled, but the story reminded me of my change from a friend of the friendless to a yokel-basher. By becoming a career girl in the big city, was I overcoming the accident of my birth or was I trying to create for myself a life that was unnatural? Helen Poltrain must have seen the distress on my face because she suddenly showed great concern.

"I didn't mean to upset you with my mother's story," she said.

"No, no, it's all right. It just got me to thinking."

"Well, I shouldn't be taking up so much of your time. Ever since you called, I've tried to think of some extra information I could add to the letter I wrote you. All I could come up with was the exact date of the baby's birth: August 18, 1988. I remember waiting up for my mother and watching the news. That was the night that the first George Bush accepted the Republican Party nomination and said, 'Read my lips: no new taxes.' Yesterday I looked up the date in the library. Other than that, all I can recommend is that you visit Hawley Huskins."

"You said in your letter that Mr. Huskins was an eccentric. Can you be more specific?"

"I was being polite. He's crazy. He collects every piece of junk he can get his hands on. To call him a packrat would be an understatement. After all these years, I'm still not sure how he makes a living. Selling junk maybe and maybe some moonshine. I just don't know."

"Do you think he'll talk to me?"

"Oh, he'll talk. I don't know, though, if his talk will be worth listening to."

"But it's all I've got, you think?"

"He had more contact with the couple than anyone else, even if it was only for a week. I don't think he knows about the flying baby. My mother didn't tell him."

I thanked Helen Poltrain and headed back to my car. As I was opening the door, she called out to me one last time.

"Miss Watkins!"

I turned back towards the house.

She hesitated, then said, "I hope it's true."

I nodded. "So do I."

Chapter 5

The Second Letter

Hawley Huskins lived at the end of a road that could hardly be called a road. I am sure that if I had checked my contract, the car rental company would have prohibited driving on such a road. It was a deeply eroded dirt path with potholes that hadn't been filled in years. There were long chasms that stretched completely across the road so that they couldn't be avoided. I was on the verge of deciding that I had taken a wrong turn when, after four and three-tenths miles of motorist's hell, I spotted signs of human life.

There was no question that I had found the right place. The first of Mr. Huskins' collections that I came upon was eight dead, Chevy Malibus, stripped of engines and tires, rusted and otherwise beaten by the weather. I felt like putting blinkers on the headlights of my own car, for fear it would turn and run at the sight. I wondered if this road psychically lured Chevy Malibus to their death, leaving their drivers in the hands of the mad Hawley Huskins.

Beyond the Malibus was a vast graveyard of automobiles, a rotting museum of vehicular corpses, ravaged with a 'surgical precision' reminiscent of the Colorado cattle mutilations. The area was almost devoid of plant life, as if Mr. Huskins was using automobiles instead of herbicides as weed killers.

Past the automobiles I encountered an ex-meadow covered with refrigerators so broken and ruined that you wouldn't worry about allowing your children to play among them. Then came a field filled with eighty years of farm implements. The curators of the Smithsonian would have been delirious with joy to have discovered such a treasure trove of Americana—except for one problem: Hawley Huskins had allowed these relics to rust and fall apart. He had made no attempt whatsoever to care for them or preserve them. It was as if he was thumbing his nose at history. As I bounced past mounds of once salvageable, but now useless, bathtubs, bicycles, toilets, bed frames, guitars, water heaters and yes, there they were, kitchen sinks, it occurred to me that Hawley Huskins might actually turn out to be a demented art student who had given up his loft in Soho or his atelier in Paris and turned this forgotten corner of the United States into an enormous work of conceptual art, a symbolic presentation of his contempt for our modern material existence.

Around a bend, between a forest of barbed wire and a disturbing cluster of moss-covered mannequins, I suddenly found myself face-to-face with Mr. Huskins' house. My poor Chevy Malibu was immediately assaulted by an incredibly large dog of a breed with which I was not only unfamiliar, but which I could not have imagined. It looked like a wolf that had been cross-bred with an ogre from a nightmarish fairy tale. I fumbled while trying to find the button to raise the window of my car. The beast leapt right at me and my only thought was that I had survived this perilous drive only to die in the grip of a rabid monster.

At the last second, a voice called out from the porch of the wood-framed house.

"Honupcoy," it sounded like. The beast froze, gave me a pleasant, puppy-like turn of the head and trotted back to the porch.

At first I couldn't make out the source of the voice, so cluttered with junk was the porch and the area surrounding it. Then I saw him. He was sitting in a rocking chair, a vast tumor of a man with chins beyond counting. He was not a former art student. With one hand he patted The Beast on the head; with the other he motioned for me to join him.

I gave my heart a few seconds to recover from its brush with death, then left the sanctuary of my car and strode past what appeared to be a ball of twist-ties five feet in diameter, up a questionable set of stairs and onto the porch. Hawley Huskins pointed to a second rocking chair and I sat down. He turned to the side and spat out a stream of ugly red liquid.

"Hope Freddie didn't scare you too much," he said.

I dismissed the notion with a wave of my hand.

We stared at each other for about twenty seconds. Then he

asked, "Passing through?"

In more than three years of traveling around Yokelland, I don't believe I had ever heard such a stupid question. Here I had just traveled four and three-tenths hellish miles on a mock road, a dead-end that led nowhere but to his house, and Hawley Huskins asks me if I am "Passing through."

"Yup," I replied, as blandly as I could, "just passing through."

Hawley Huskins seemed satisfied. "Where you come from?"

"New York," was on the tip of my tongue, but I caught myself. "North Carolina."

Hawley Huskins shook his head in amazement. "You sure have come a long way." Another stream of red liquid went flying over the porch railing.

"Where'd you get all of your stuff?" I asked, nodding in the general direction of his various "collections."

"Roadsides mostly. People know me around these parts. If something's finished being used, it finds me."

"Why do you do it?"

"Keeps everything in one place." Zap went another stream of red liquid. Until this point I had assumed he was spitting out used chewing tobacco, but he had already spewed out so much that now I worried that it was actually some vile secretion that his body was producing. I began to feel queasy. The time had come to make my move.

I sensed that tactful behavior would be wasted on Hawley Huskins, so I plunged right in. "Do you remember a couple that rented a shack from you about twenty years ago? The woman gave birth here."

Mr. Huskins stopped rocking, thought a moment, then resumed. "Sure do. Strange couple. Looked just like each other. Funny how some folks likes a spouse that's like looking in a mirror."

"Kind of like Mick Jagger and Bianca, huh?"

"Who?"

"Famous rock and roll singer."

"Never heard of her."

"Did you see the baby after it was born?"

"Nope. Couple skipped out in the dead of night. Owed me rent too."

"Sorry to hear that."

"They did pay me back about a year later."

This time it was me who stopped rocking. "I beg your pardon?"

"About a year later, a letter came addressed to me. Opened it up and there was eight one-dollar bills, exactly what they owed me."

"Was there a note in it?"

"Yup."

"What did it say?"

Zoom. Still more red liquid cleared the porch railing.

"Don't know. Only thing I can read is my name."

"Then how did you know that it was from the people with the baby?"

"Only folks who owed me eight dollars."

Fair enough, I thought. What I'd give, though, to have that note. But why would an illiterate save a letter that was nineteen years old? Then I looked around at the barbed wire, the toilets, the kitchen sinks. On the other hand, why would this particular illiterate throw it away?

"Do you still have the letter?"

"S'pose so."

"Can I see it?"

"Don't see why not."

Mr. Huskins stopped rocking and made elaborate preparations to rise. First he expelled a huge, revolting wad of red muck. Then he planted his feet, grasped tightly the arms of the chair and leaned forward until he reached what years of practice had evidently taught him was the ideal angle. He pushed down and slowly rose, his cheeks and jowls turning bright red from the effort. He took hold of a wooden post and said, "Follow me."

Instinctively, I planted my feet, slowly leaned forward and pushed myself up with great care.

There were four steps leading down to the ground. Mr. Huskins took each one like it was a separate journey, carefully testing his balance before he moved on to the next one. Once he reached the ground, he seemed more confident. Joined by The Beast, who rose as ponderously as his master, Hawley Huskins headed around the house to the back. Halfway there he stopped so suddenly that I almost bumped into him.

"That's the shack where they lived," he said, pointing towards an empty field.

I couldn't imagine what he was talking about. Then I realized that he was referring to a pile of wood about seventy-five yards off. It must have collapsed in a storm at least ten years earlier. Only Hawley Huskins would think to refer to it still as a shack.

Behind the house was a veritable cathedral of animal bones—at least I hoped they were *animal* bones. Behind this monument to past generations were two large barns. One of them really was a barn, complete with cows and chickens and turkeys and a couple of enormous swine. I could see that Mr. Huskins was self-sufficient enough to not require too much of an outside income.

The second barn was another story. Here was another manifestation of his desire to "keep everything in one place." Laid out in careful rows, as if in a shop for things you wouldn't buy, were bottle caps, string, wire, broken pieces of plastic, newspapers, cardboard boxes, shards of glass, newels, old shoes, bubble gum wrappers, broken scissors, disposable pens long ago disposed of and much more. Threading our way through the aisles, we came at last to an unboxed six-foot-high double stack of envelopes: a lifetime of mail. Most of it was bills and advertisements.

Hawley Huskins studied the stacks, apparently estimating the dates of the letters by the extent to which they had yellowed. With a surprisingly delicate motion, he pushed up against one stack with one arm and, using two fingers, wriggled out a single envelope.

"Yup, this is it."

I was impressed not only by his memory, but by his filing system. "May I look at it?"

Instead of handing it over, he held it up in front of me. It was addressed to "Hawley Huskins/Mosquito Lick, Kentucky." The handwriting was neat and confident, not at all what one would expect of an uneducated yokel. There was no return address, but there was a postmark from Tennessee. Mr. Huskins pulled the envelope away before I could make out the town.

He lifted the back flap and peered inside.

"Note's still there."

"Will you sell me the letter?" I asked, impulsively.

Hawley Huskins winced as if I had asked him to break up a

complete set of *National Geographics* or Liberty Head quarters.

"I'll give you ten dollars."

His look of pain vanished. I quickly extracted a ten-dollar bill from my pocketbook before he changed his mind. I forced the money into his left hand and snatched the envelope from his right. I glanced immediately at the postmark: Kilgore, Tennessee. All I could think about was to get to my car, look up Kilgore on my road map and read the letter inside the envelope.

First I had to appear civil, as Hawley Huskins, in his leisurely way, led me back outside and around to the front of the house. Before climbing the stairs to the porch, he spat out another stream of red liquid and surveyed his domain. An expression of contentment spread across his face.

"Good life, don't you think?"

Sure, I thought, if you like sitting on your porch and staring at the insides of discarded toilets.

"No doubt about it," I said. "I guess I best be moving on."

"If you must. Thanks for stopping by."

On the way back to the car, I felt annoyed that I, who was well-educated and had a good job, was spiritually tormented, while Hawley Huskins, whose legacy to the world would be a ready-made landfill, was completely at peace. But as soon as I got behind the wheel I remembered the letter in my hand and burned with excitement. I turned the Chevy Malibu around, waved a final good-bye to Sri Huskins and started back on the path leading through the circles of purgatory to what passed for modern civilization. As quickly as the Malibu's suspension would allow, I left behind the barbed wire and moss-covered mannequins, the kitchen sinks, the water heaters, the bathtubs, the ploughs and the refrigerators. Once I was safely past the dead automobiles and out of sight of Hawley Huskins' house, I stopped the car and pulled out my road map of Kentucky and Tennessee.

"Tennessee Index: Cities and Towns." Second column: "Kilgore 584....... G-11." The town had as many people as my freshman English class at Columbia. I found G-11 and there was Kilgore, a dot on scenic highway 93, one mile east of mildly scenic highway 35 in Calhoun County. I traced the route from Mosquito Lick and discovered that it was about 86 miles away. I was tempted to drive straight through, but the sun was close to setting, so I decided to find a motel in nearby Haresville on the Cumberland River, and then get an early start in the morning.

I took the sacred envelope in both hands and studied it. It was postmarked August 18, 1989, one year after the baby's birth. Slowly I pulled out the letter, fearful that its contents would be disappointing. The letter was written in the same neat script as the address. It read:

Dear Mr. Huskins,

Sorry it took so long to pay off our debt to you. We've had a hard time, but now we have a few dollars to spare. If you see the midwife who helped us, please ask her to pray for us and tell her— He's still doing it.

I felt the proverbial chill go up my spine. "He's still doing it." In 1989, a one-year-old baby boy was flying through the air in Calhoun County, Tennessee, U.S.A.

I spent that evening in a moldy, decrepit motel room in Haresville, Kentucky, the kind of room Hawley Huskins would feel comfortable in if he ever had to leave his home. I didn't mind it, even though I was too excited to sleep. I read and re-read the letter endlessly. It was unsigned, so I still had no leads to the family's real name. I was relieved that the couple had allowed their son to live. It seemed less likely that they would have killed it after twelve months of becoming attached. A couple of details in the letter provoked my interest. The dashes in the last line and the capitalization of the H showed that the author was not that well-educated. And yet he or she had correctly included the apostrophes in "we've" and "He's." I deduced that the letter writer had been a good student, but had been forced to drop out of school for some reason, probably because of the pregnancy, although not necessarily.

The couple seemed to be on the run, not only because of Violet Poltrain's description of their nervousness, but because the letter said they had had a hard time since the birth of their child. That would be less likely if they had returned to the bosom of a loving family. I was willing to bet, though, that they were from Tennessee, although not from Calhoun County. They probably fled across the state line to give birth, then fled back after the baby turned out to be supernatural. I couldn't imagine them going back to their home county, but I could see them seeking familiar countryside. I wanted to believe that they had settled in Kilgore and that they were still there, but I had to admit that it was unlikely. It was possible that Kilgore was nothing more than a mailbox they dropped a letter in while on the move. Still, somehow they had managed to earn a few dollars, a few extra dollars at that. I asked myself what I would do if I had a baby who would suddenly fly through the air without warning. Would I stay on the road, moving from town to town? Not likely. More likely, I would seek out an extremely remote home, even more remote than Hawley Huskins' shack, somewhere where no one would even know that I had a baby.

Trying to put myself inside the minds of this frightened couple gave me an idea. Instead of waiting until morning to drive to Kilgore, why not do as they had done and leave in the middle of the night. I had paid my motel bill upon arrival, so I was free to go whenever I pleased. I packed my traveling bag, hopped in the car and headed back to the dirt road leading to Hawley Huskins' place. When I got there, I tried to imagine what this young couple must have felt on that dark, dark night twenty years earlier.

It wasn't hard to recreate their fear. Just being alone on this isolated country road at two in the morning was pretty scary. At least they had each other. But of course they had more than each other. They had a strange little being, their own flesh and blood, whom they couldn't understand or control. I headed east again, feeling terribly vulnerable, a young woman by myself in the middle of the night. I had visions of insane characters from *Deliverance* or an Erskine Caldwell novel springing up from the bushes. I pushed my foot on the pedal as the couple—what were their phony names? Tom and Tammy—as Tom and Tammy must have done. They were speeding away from Violet Poltrain, the only person who knew their secret, and from the terror of what had happened in the shack. And yet the terror was right there with them in the car.

But what was so terrible about it really? Wasn't it a little exciting in a way to have a baby who could do what no other baby could do, what no other adult could do, for that matter? I eased up on the gas and relaxed. I drove by my motel and kept going.

Wasn't it possible that that first night they were struck by the awesomeness of it all? Wasn't it possible that they looked down at their innocent little sleeping baby, gazed into each other's eyes, held each other's hands and felt blessed? Then I remembered a line from the letter they had sent to Hawley Huskins: "Pray for us ..." After a year of living with a baby who could fly, they were still frightened. I hunkered down over the steering wheel and ground out the miles as fast as I could, checking constantly for any sign of headlights in my rearview mirror.

Fourteen miles past Haresville I saw a sign pointing toward Tennessee, so I turned right on to the next highway and headed south. Twelve miles later I crossed the state line and imagined that Tom and Tammy, at this point in their flight, must have felt a false sense of relief that passed quickly when they realized they still had no place to go. Winding my way through mountainous terrain that I guessed was dramatically beautiful in daylight, I began to feel very tired. It was all I could do to keep my eyes open.

I was startled into alertness by a speck of light in my rearview mirror. As it grew larger, my heart seemed to grow larger too. I gripped the steering wheel tighter. I couldn't decide if I should speed up or slow down. I drove around a bend and the light disappeared. For a full minute I saw no more sign of a car behind me. I had almost convinced myself that the driver had turned off when suddenly I was blinded by bright lights filling my side view mirror. I was so shocked I swerved. Then I slowed down. A pickup truck whizzed by me. I thought I saw the driver glance at me and do a double take, but I wasn't sure. As soon as he disappeared from my view, I turned off at the first opportunity.

I found myself on a narrow highway heading toward Grimms State Park and back in the direction of Kentucky. I took a right onto unpaved Buffalowood Fork Road and crept into Big Smoky National Recreation Area. Surely Tom and Tammy, twenty years ago, exhausted and fearing discovery, would have done much the same. I found a dirt road leading into the forest, followed it for a mile and pulled over. I turned off the car engine, rolled down the window slightly and listened. All I could hear were insects and the beating of my heart. I rolled the window back up, locked the doors and pushed my seat back. How had Tom and Tammy felt that night? Frightened, as I was? And what of the baby? Was he banging against the roof? I was afraid to fall asleep, afraid someone would find me. But I was so tired that I fell asleep immediately.

I awoke before dawn. Nothing terrible had happened to me. I was parked beside an abandoned mine that was covered with moss and overgrown with vines. I relieved myself behind a bush and then turned the car around and drove back to Buffalowood Fork Road.

I still felt nervous in the predawn light, but I also felt proud of myself, as if I had survived a night in a haunted house. Forty minutes later I arrived in Milltown (population 3,029, said the sign). Sitting over a cup of coffee and a plate of fried eggs at Delilah's Foodette, I enjoyed a sense of accomplishment, not to mention relief. It occurred to me that for the first time since I left my motel room, I was not in tune with Tom and Tammy. They could not have simply dropped into a diner for breakfast, not with a seven-hour-old baby who might vault over the waitress' head without warning. And, if it took a full year to pay off their eight-dollar debt to Hawley Huskins, they might not have been able to afford fried eggs and a cup of coffee anyway. I decided to end my attempt to put myself in their shoes. With pleasure, I reverted to the more comfortable role of investigative reporter.

But this case was different from all of my others. Whether I was on the track of a UFO or a toad fall or a poltergeist, my modus operandi was generally the same. I knew what had happened, I knew who had seen it, and all I had to do was interview the relevant parties, who were almost always eager to talk.

This time, however, I was trying to pick up a trail that had vanished nineteen years earlier. I was also trying to find people who didn't want to be found. It wouldn't do to chat up local policemen and reporters as I usually did. I couldn't even let it be known that I was a columnist for the *New York Insider*. Word would get around quickly and, if Tom and Tammy and their twenty-year-old son were still in the area, it might scare them away. I needed a cover.

I recalled my last visit to Tennessee two years earlier. It was another case of unexpected objects falling from the sky, although this time there was less uncertainty about their source than there was with the frogs that landed in the Shreveport schoolyard.

One evening, at 8:53 P.M. to be exact, a rare book dealer named DeWayne Ripley was sitting in the living room of his Memphis home, reading a new translation of Camus' *The Stranger*, when he heard a tremendous roar, followed by the cracking of wood and a loud thump. He put down his Camus, opened the door to his bedroom and discovered that the room was filled with dust and that there was a hole in the roof. When the dust settled, he found a twenty-five-pound chunk of greenish ice with brown lumps inside lying beside his bed. Mr. Ripley, a bespectacled widower, called the police, who appropriated the ice chunk and turned it over to the chemistry department at Memphis State University. Mr. Ripley was interviewed by the local newspapers, who published photographs of the ice chunk and the roof. The chemists at Memphis State did not make public their report. In the meantime, Mr. Ripley paid to have his roof rebuilt.

Exactly two weeks after the first incident, this time at 9:02 P.M., DeWayne Ripley was sitting in his living room re-reading a first edition of *The Last Puritan* by George Santayana, when there was another roar, crash and thud. This time the unwanted visitor landed right in his living room, missing Mr. Ripley by a mere ten feet. When the dust cleared, there was another twenty-five-pound chunk of greenish ice with brown lumps inside. The local press pressured the police and the university. Finally, the Federal Aviation Administration admitted that the two frozen specimens were human waste from the leaky toilet of an airplane used for Delta Airlines' regular flight from Cincinnati to Memphis. Mr. Ripley was re-interviewed by the local press before and after the admission. The story was also reported by a stringer for Reuters. His story was picked up on the international wire and, before long, reporters from Japan, Italy, Great Britain, Australia and the Philippines were calling the besieged book dealer and requesting interviews.

Even though there was no mystery in the case, I couldn't resist the story. Besides, there was always the possibility that either the chemists were wrong in their analysis or that the FAA had been hasty in their assessment of blame. Perhaps DeWayne Ripley had a secret enemy with a macabre sense of humor.

Unfortunately, by the time I got to Memphis, Mr. Ripley, a reserved and private man, was sick of reporters and refused to be interviewed ever again. I was not prepared to give up so easily. Recalling a scene from *The Big Sleep*, I posed as a rare book collector and visited Mr. Ripley's shop. After an hour of charming, bookish conversation, he took me to lunch, opened up and told me about the "shit attacks" as he called them and about the subsequent onslaught of journalists, which he referred to as "Shit Attacks 2." It made a great column for the *Insider*. To assuage my guilt for having deceived him, I made DeWayne Ripley the innocent good guy and I saved my acidic comments for the bozo journalists who had descended on him with their stupid questions.

CHAPTER 6

CALHOUN COUNTY

Now, sitting at Delilah's Foodette in Milltown, Tennessee, I needed to come up with a similarly effective ruse. I needed something that would allow me to be snoopy without arousing the distrust and hostility that would naturally come my way as a journalist from New York. Clearly I had to fall back on my North Carolina roots. After all, my home state was only 175 miles away. But how could I get away with asking people if they had ever seen a boy flying through the air?

It came to me in a flash. I was a folklorist from the University of North Carolina collecting southern tales of the supernatural—particularly modern tales.

I quickly paid my bill and then filled up my gas tank. I was on my way out of Milltown and headed toward Kilgore when I realized that I was being too hasty. I didn't know the first thing about Tennessee folklore. I turned around and found my way to the Milltown Public Library. There I spent three hours immersing myself in Tennessee folktales, tall tales and superstitions. The shelves were overflowing with material about Daniel Boone and Davy Crockett. I did not find it relevant or even interesting, but I skimmed it anyway so that I wouldn't appear completely ignorant of local history and mythology. I also memorized the tale of The Bell Witch, the story of a ghost who wanted to marry a living woman, and I skimmed various accounts of headless horsemen, enchanted forests and haunted houses.

More secure in my guise as a folklorist, I returned to the road, drove south for six miles and turned left onto the Clement C. Kilgore Highway, which took me into Kilgore. A sign read, "Welcome to

Kilgore: Appalachian Soul, American Spirit." I drove through town so quickly that I had to double back and make another pass. As I cruised the downtown streets, so many people waved at me that I thought they mistook me for someone else. In contrast to Mosquito Lick or Milltown or any of the other towns I had driven through, Kilgore seemed to be the ideal small town. The courthouse, the school, even the welfare office and the jail, were perfectly clean and freshly painted. A group of mentally handicapped people was watering the flower garden in front of the courthouse. I watched one of them return his equipment to a building in the middle of town and discovered that it was the Center for the Mentally Challenged. Instead of hiding their simpler citizens in a barricaded institution on the outskirts of town, the good people of Kilgore incorporated them into the community and gave them worthwhile work.

I also noticed two diners, a Baptist church, a small library and a post office—*the* post office where my precious letter had been mailed. There was no movie theater and no gas station.

As a journalist, I would have begun my investigation with a visit to the local newspaper or perhaps to the police station. But as a folklorist I decided it would be more appropriate to start at the Calhoun County Library.

The librarian on duty was a stout young man of about my age with a neatly trimmed beard and mustache and a mischievous smile. I explained to him that I was a Ph.D. candidate at the University of North Carolina researching my doctoral thesis on "Supernatural Tales of the Old and New South."

"Any supernatural beings ever show up here in Kilgore?" I asked.

"Sure have. Dick Cheney stayed here a couple years ago. If ever there was a guy who lived outside of normal reality it was him."

"Must have been scary," I countered. "What was he doing here?"

"He was staying with Clement Kilgore, the senator."

"The same Clement Kilgore who gave his name to this road?"

"No, that was the senator's father, Congressman Kilgore. The Congressman was a bit insulted when they named the road after him. Said it was typical they should name the crookedest road in the county after a politician."

"Pretty nice town you've got here. Must be the envy of every small town in the state."

"You can thank the Kilgores for that. They've always known how to take care of their own."

"What else can you tell me about local folklore?"

"Not much, to tell you the truth. I'm from Knoxville. I took this job three years ago. The person you want to talk to is Ethel Wilton. She's the county historian and the president of the historical society. She even wrote a book about it: *Lost Pieces of the Calhoun County Puzzle*. You can pick up a copy at Jellico's General Store."

Jellico's General Store. It sounded wonderfully "downhome," something the readers of the *New York Insider* would relish. In fact, it was a typical convenience store straight out of Anywhere, U.S.A. Instead of jars of pickled hog's feet and grits stew with grits sauce, I found sliced white bread and frozen pizzas. Still, across from the cash register, next to *Better Homes and Gardens*, *Field and Stream* and the *National Enquirer*, was half a shelf of books and pamphlets of local interest. I grabbed a copy of *Lost Pieces of the Calhoun County Puzzle*, as well as a county road map.

Because I'm used to working on a deadline during my trips into Yokelland, I tend to work straight through until I'm about to collapse. It was exactly that point that I had reached as I left Jellico's General Store. Except for the two or three hours of sleep I had managed in the forest, I had been going non-stop for more than thirty hours.

I found my way to the Kilgore Inn, paid for a room, took a shower and collapsed on the bed. As tired as I was, I was too curious about *Lost Pieces* to go right to sleep.

It turned out to be a sprawling 623-page hodge-podge of family histories, histories of buildings and churches, randomly reprinted documents and semiliterate nineteenth-century diary entries. One chapter, entitled "Negroes," dealt with the history of race relations. In the case of Calhoun County this meant the white people allowing the black people to work at the brickyard outside of town around the turn of the century and then lynching them if they talked back or smiled the wrong way at a white woman. Included in a photo essay of "Quaint Customs of Bygone Days" was a sign above Main Street reading, "Nigger, don't let the sun set on you."

In the folklore chapter, there was no mention of a flying child, although the county did seem to have more than its share of haunted houses and bewitched country lanes. I fell asleep expecting ghosts to inhabit my dreams, but when I was awakened by my wrist alarm, the only image I could retrieve was plates sneaking across a kitchen counter and crawling into cupboards as my mother dashed into the room trying to catch them.

The combination of this unsettling image and the useless mumbo-jumbo of Ethel Wilton's magnum opus put me in a dark mood. My search seemed to be leading nowhere. My only clue was a nineteen-year-old letter with a Kilgore postmark. I had no evidence that the family still lived in the area and no evidence that the boy was still alive, much less still flying, if he really ever had. And what was I doing pursuing such a longshot story anyway? My practical side told me to give up and return to some easy UFO sighting or a crocodile appearing in a swimming pool. But my little girl side, the part of me that wanted to believe, won out.

My only lead was Ethel Wilton. Fortunately, her address and phone number were right there on the copyright page of her book. On the phone, she sounded much friendlier and livelier than the smug, white-haired old guard who usually protect a county's history as if it were their own personal property.

"Supernatural tales?" she exclaimed. "Sounds like fun. Why don't you join me and my husband Claude for dinner? Claude has kind of a weird sense of humor, but he's all right."

I babbled a bit about not wanting to intrude, but Ethel insisted, and I agreed to go to their house at six o'clock. I was about to say goodbye and hang up when I was struck by an idea.

One time I had ventured into Humboldt County in northwestern California after a number of sightings of "a large, hairy beast." Because the area was inhabited primarily by hippies and bohemians, I was able to turn the piece into a series of comic encounters, i.e. "I had trouble finding anyone who wasn't a large, hairy beast." At one point I was given the following directions to find the home of one of the witnesses: "Drive east on county road 4057 about six miles. When you see a white rag hanging from a tree on your left, park your car and walk straight into the forest. After about twenty yards you'll find a path. Follow the path for about two hundred yards and Tree's yurt will be on the right." I found Tree and his yurt. We talked for a half hour about the large, hairy beast, as well as about astrophysics, which had been Tree's specialty before he had quit his teaching position at the University of California and retired to the forest. As I prepared to leave, I told him, "I don't believe I've ever met an American who lived so far away from civilization."

"That's nothing," said Tree. "You should visit my neighbor down the path." He pointed to a narrow opening between the trees. I did visit his neighbor, who directed me to another path and another yurt. By the time I got back to Tree, his clearing seemed like suburbia.

Recalling this incident, I blurted out to Ethel Wilton, "By the way, there's one more subject I'm interested in. It doesn't have to do with my Ph.D. thesis, but I've also been researching people who live in very remote areas, places you can't get to by car. Do you know of any such people or places here in Calhoun County?"

"Offhand, I can't think of any place you can't get to with a four-wheel drive. Maybe my son would know. He works for social services. Before the budget cutbacks he made home visits to everyone who asked for public assistance. I'll invite him over tonight and you can ask him."

I was back in good spirits by the time I arrived at the Wilton residence. Even though I still had no useful information, I sensed that at least I was talking to the right people.

The Wiltons lived in a wood-frame house on the outskirts of Kilgore. Claude, a tall, rangy, bald-topped man in his sixties, met me at the door. He blocked my entrance while he looked me up and down. "Well, you're a spunky young thing, aren't you?" he said at last. I was wearing one of my "spunky" outfits, a full-length dress with a tight top. My hair was cut in bangs. Appearing "cute" was one of the more important tricks of the trade I had learned, like driving a Chevy Malibu.

Having passed Claude Wilton's inspection, I was allowed to pass into the house, where I was greeted by his wife, Ethel, and their only son, Doc.

"Are you a doctor?" I asked the son, a bit confused.

Doc Wilton, short and slight, rolled his eyes as if he had been asked this question for the four millionth time. His parents looked away in embarrassment.

"No, they named me Doc when I was born."

"We thought it would give him an air of respectability," explained Claude. "We thought it would force him to be wise."

"Instead," added Ethel, "he grew up to be a wise guy, like his dad." Ethel had the appearance of one of those white-haired small-town busybodies whom I dreaded, but her demeanor was more like that of a warm Jewish grandmother. She fussed over me for a few minutes and then led me straight to the dinner table.

From a Tennessee county historian, I expected a meal of parboiled squirrels, hominy and buttered turnips, but, as with the shelves at Jellico's General Store, I was to be surprised. The Wiltons, it seemed, although born and bred in Calhoun County, had lived for ten years in Southern California, where Claude had worked as a design engineer in the aerospace industry. Ethel had studied cooking.

Waiting for me on the dinner table was a dazzling array of southern French *hors-d'oeuvres:* aubergine caviar, quiche *provençale,* celery with anchovy cream and *petites pâtes* with minced ham and veal. I had planned to bully the conversation in the direction of flying children as quickly as possible, but the *hors-d'oeuvres* were so delicious that I was thrown off guard. Claude and Doc pumped me with questions about my life as an academic and I was forced to fabricate many more details than I had planned. Fortunately, my hours of study earlier in the day and my legitimate North Carolina upbringing allowed me to carry it off.

My familiarity with *Lost Pieces of the Calhoun County Puzzle* delighted Ethel and took me through the cod *bouillabaisse.* Finally, during the bass *au gratin á la Salonaise,* we got around to the subject of supernatural tales. But it turned out that none of the Wiltons had any stories to add to the ones I had already skimmed in Ethel's book.

"Ever heard any rumors of strange objects flying through space?" I asked as casually as possible.

"Strange objects?" asked Ethel. "Like what?"

"Oh, you know, dogs, cats ... people."

The Wiltons frowned and shrugged. "Not really," said Claude. Ethel and Doc agreed.

I was unable to mask my disappointment. Concerned, they

tried to be helpful.

"We've had plenty of UFO reports," offered Doc, "blinking lights and that sort of thing. But this area has a long history of moonshine. If you ask around enough, you'll probably find dozens of people who've seen pink elephants flying through space."

Ethel Wilton urged me to indulge in dessert: almond croquettes, fried cakes with rum, and an extraordinary sweet spinach pie topped with tangerine slices. Didn't you want to know about people who live off the beaten path?" she urged. "Nobody in the county would know better than Doc."

"Yes. Your mother told me you used to make home visits to welfare recipients."

"I also worked on the census. I did the follow-ups on people who didn't answer by mail."

"So, are there any people whose homes are so remote that they can't be reached by car?"

Doc Wilton knitted his brows and thought for a while. "It gets pretty funky up by Cullowassee Creek. There's families holed up in all sorts of nooks and crannies out there, but I can't think of any that don't have some kind of car path leading to their door, even if that door belongs to an abandoned car. Not only that, but the deer and coon hunters go just about everywhere with their ATVs."

"What about out by Misty Hollow?" asked Claude.

"Yeah, they're really weird out there," added Ethel.

"I suppose it's possible," said Doc. "There's no telling what goes on in Misty Hollow, especially in the direction of Dark Mountain."

I leaned forward in anticipation. "What do you mean when you say 'they're really weird'?"

"One time I did a home visit up there and this one woman had just bought a brand new vacuum cleaner. Only problem was she didn't have electricity."

"There's really only two families out by Misty Hollow," explained Claude, "the Slagels and the Jukes. They've been intermarrying for so many generations that they're all a little strange. A lot of kids have fathers and uncles who are one and the same, if you know what I mean."

"They've all got loaded rifles, too," added Doc, "and lots of guns. The state prison is on the other side of the mountains, down in Petros. Whenever someone escapes, they head for the back country in Calhoun County. That's where James Earl Ray, the guy who killed Martin Luther King, escaped from. But there's been far worse than him."

"That's only an excuse," said Claude. "Those Slagels and Jukes are just plain mean. Who knows what secrets they're hiding up there? Remember that gravel runway they built?"

"Drug smuggling?" I asked.

"Must have been. Anyone who knows the back roads could get from that strip to highway 75 without being noticed."

"Do you think they were bringing in cocaine from other countries or could they have been flying out homegrown marijuana?"

Claude and Doc shrugged. "Could be both," replied Doc.

"How long have the Slagels and the Jukes been living in these parts?"

"The Slagels have been around since the 1820s," answered Ethel, "but the Jukes didn't arrive for another fifty years."

"I'd like to meet them," I ventured. "I'll bet the older family members are full of good stories."

Ethel and Claude looked dubious, but Doc was more encouraging. "I could take you up there," he said. "I went to school with Lard Slagel, so they all know me. They might talk to an outsider if I was with you."

"When can we do it?"

"If I got all my work done in the morning, I suppose we could go out tomorrow afternoon." Doc did some silent calculating and then added, "I could pick you up at the Kilgore Inn at about 1:00 P.M."

Back in my motel room, my mind was abuzz with possibilities. Could it be that the secrets that the Slagels and the Jukes were hiding were even more unusual than incest and drug smuggling? Could they be harboring a twenty-year-old boy who flies? I recalled Hawley Huskins' description of Tom and Tammy: that they "looked like each other." Perhaps they were brother and sister, either Slagels or Jukes. But given the rumors about the two families, why would they have bothered to run away? Although I was still lacking hard evidence, I was growing more confident that someone in Calhoun

County knew something about Tom and Tammy and their child, even if that something wasn't that the boy could fly.

I looked again at the letter I had purchased from Hawley Huskins. "… Tell her—he's still doing it." I studied the handwriting and wondered if someone in Kilgore would recognize it. Yet it was a difficult matter to pursue without appearing to be a detective and instantly arousing suspicion. If Tom and Tammy had applied for welfare or filled out any other official papers, their signatures would be on file. But they were unlikely to have done anything that would call attention to themselves. I still leaned to the theory that they had disappeared into the wilderness and built themselves as self-sufficient a life as possible. But I also believed that a visit to Misty Hollow was worth the effort since, as I discovered from the county map I had bought at Jellico's General Store, it was on the edge of the largest roadless area in the state.

The next morning I got up early and took a gamble. I paid a visit to the Kilgore post office on Court Street and asked if any of the postal workers had been employed there back in 1989. Eugene Snaith emerged from behind a display of the Declaration of Independence and the Constitution. He was a weaselly-looking man in his late fifties. He glared at me with just the sort of suspicious look I had feared. I showed him my envelope, although I kept the letter in my purse. I told him that my mother, on her deathbed, had asked me to track down the people who had sent her this envelope, but that I didn't know their names. I asked him if he recognized the handwriting or if there was anything else he could tell me by studying the postmark. He studied it for fifteen seconds and said, "All I can tell you is that it was mailed on August 18, 1989." Then he handed it back to me and left the room.

I tried to look at the bright side of this encounter: at least I had learned that the postmark wasn't a forgery. And perhaps Mr. Snaith was a good introduction to my upcoming visit to the Slagels and Jukes, with their reputation for being closemouthed. I considered other avenues I could pursue—marriage records, schools, truant officers—but none of them seemed worth the effort. Instead, I wandered in and out of shops on Main Street, observing the local population. Was it possible that one of these people, innocently going about their business, was really Tom or Tammy? They'd be in their thirties by now. Or maybe one of these young men, revving his Harley-Davidson or hauling trash, was the flying boy himself. Perhaps, as he had grown, he had learned to control his talent and was able to hide it. My Lois Lane fantasies resurfaced. I returned to the Kilgore Inn without having picked up a single clue.

CHAPTER 7

MISTY HOLLOW

Doc Wilton picked me up in his Jeep Grand Cherokee at one o'clock sharp.

"This boy," I said, "the one that you went to school with, Lard Slagel, I imagine by his nickname that he must be pretty fat."

"Not at all. He's muscular, solid as a rock; Lard is his real name. They named him Lard after his father's favorite food."

"Mister Slagel's favorite food is lard?"

"Yes. Of course all the Slagel boys have names starting with L: Lard, Lem, Lige and Lavern. They used Gs for the girls: Georgia, Gilda and Granny."

"Granny?"

"Yes, she's about twenty-one years old now. I always had a crush on her, ever since we were little. I thought we were fated to fall in love because we were both saddled with names it would take a long time to grow into. But four years ago she up and married Eb Juke. I think she's still the prettiest girl in the county."

I was touched by the bitterness in his voice.

"You know, Doc, I thought the reason you volunteered to take me to Misty Hollow was just to be helpful to a stranger. But the real reason is that you saw it as a chance to see Granny Slagel again, isn't it?"

"Granny Juke," he corrected me with continued bitterness. "Maybe it's a combination of the two."

Doc Wilton clammed up at this point. I peered out the window of the Jeep. The day had turned overcast. We passed by groves of white oak, hickory, yellow pine, American linden. The countryside was lovely, but there was a definite gloominess in the air. I imagined that the weather frequently forced the locals into dangerous fits of introspection.

About six miles east of Kilgore, we turned right onto the narrow Selma Road and cruised through rolling hills of dogwood and mountain laurel.

"It's beautiful," I murmured, admiring the patches of blooming bloodroot, trout lily and purple cress.

"It's come back pretty well over the decades. This area was cut down for lumber early in the century. Then the hills were strip-mined after World War II. That's the story of this county. The rest of the country ignores it. Then some outsider discovers we have something he can make some money on, they grab whatever they want and leave us behind to clean up the mess."

I thought I'd better let that one go without a comment, considering the nature of my own visit. At least I didn't intend to leave behind a mess.

After a few more miles, the pavement ended and we bumped along Misty Junction Road, a dirt path that followed the winding of the New River and the railroad tracks that ran alongside it. At Misty Junction we crossed the tracks and the river and headed up Misty Creek Road. As the quality of the road deteriorated, we slowed considerably. Doc carefully negotiated the crossing of various smaller creeks and branches that fed into Misty Creek. The forest was too thick to see very far, but Doc assured me that off to the right were mountains, most notably Dark Mountain and Lone Mountain.

We had been driving on dirt roads for about forty minutes and hadn't seen a car or a person the whole time. Then we suddenly emerged from an especially dense thicket and found ourselves at a primitive cul-de-sac. Five decrepit automobiles were lined up along the edges. It was a mini-version of Hawley Huskins' auto graveyard.

"Welcome to Misty Hollow," said Doc Wilton. "I suggest we get out here and walk the rest of the way."

I climbed down and noticed two dirt paths leading off to the east and the south. Both of them were just wide enough for a car.

"That one leads to the Slagels," said Doc, pointing to the east. "And that one leads to the Jukes. I suggest we start with the Slagels.

D. C. Slagel is the patriarch of the clan. If he gives you his stamp of approval, you shouldn't have much trouble with all the others."

"What does 'D. C.' stand for?" I asked.

"Nothing."

For fifty yards the path led through overhanging trees. Then the trees gave way and I found myself standing in front of a huge natural amphitheater. It was like a round valley surrounded by hills. Scattered across the hills were eight wooden houses, all of them built in an architectural style I would describe as Depression-era patchwork. It was like stepping back seventy years, except that a couple of the roofs sported satellite dishes, and several of the cars parked in front of the houses were brand new Jeeps and Hummers. At first I couldn't figure out how the cars had gotten there. The houses seemed to be separated from where we stood by a green-lined abyss. But as I looked more carefully I could see that the path we had entered on split up into a series of treacherous driveways. I understood why Doc Wilton had chosen to leave his own Jeep outside the hollow in the cul-de-sac.

Just then I heard a rifle shot, and at the same time a bullet slammed into a rock not three feet from Doc, spraying shards at our feet.

"Don't be alarmed," said Doc dryly. "That's their way of saying hello. If we were strangers, we'd leave right away." He reached into his shirt pocket and pulled out a white handkerchief. He held the handkerchief high above his head and waved it. "It'll be okay now."

Doc picked one of the driveways, and I followed him down into the hollow and back up the other side. As we approached the nearest house, a brawny young man appeared on the porch. With his left hand he was supporting a baby slung over his shoulder. In his right hand was a rifle.

"Is that you, Doc?" he called out.

"Sure is. Long time, no see, Lard."

Lard seemed genuinely pleased to see Doc, but when he saw me, his expression changed. Lust is the only word that describes the emotion conveyed by the way he stared at me. Two women came out of the house and joined him. One was about eighteen years old, the other, evidently her sister, was barely fifteen. Dark hair, pale skin. I had prepared for my visit to Misty Hollow by dressing in jeans and a loose flannel shirt. These young ladies, despite the coolness of the afternoon, wore flimsy cotton dresses that clung to their bodies. They stared at me with suspicion and jealousy.

Lard handed the baby to the older sister without saying a word to her or even looking at her. His eyes never left me. "You're pretty spunky looking, aren't you?" It must have been my bangs.

"Miss Watkins is with the University of North Carolina," explained Doc. "She's collecting supernatural tales of Tennessee. I told her your granddad might know a few."

"Could be," conceded Lard, his eyes still fixed on me. He clearly viewed me as just an appealing body. The idea that I might have some sort of personality was irrelevant.

Behind him, the sisters were squirming and oozing as if our arrival had interrupted some salacious activity and they were anxious to get back to whatever it was they had been doing.

"You go on over there," said Lard. "I'll join you in a little while." Then he shot his rifle into the air. "Now wave your handkerchief."

Doc complied. Another rifle went off in the distance. Okay, you can go now," said Lard. "See you later."

I followed Doc down another path. I didn't look back for a full minute. When I did, Lard Slagel was still staring at me.

"About this D. C. Slagel," I asked Doc, "is there anything I should know about him before I meet him, anything that would help me get in his good graces?"

Doc glanced back at me as if my innocence was a matter of concern. "He's probably killed more people than anyone in the history of Calhoun County, and that's some competition he's been up against. Back in the late thirties he shot to death two men he said were poaching on his land. The judge gave him the choice of going to jail or joining the army. D. C. joined the army. When the U.S. entered World War II, he fought all over Europe, always volunteering for the most dangerous assignments. He earned some big medals for bravery. Once he took out a nest of sixty Germans single-handedly. As soon as the European front was under control, he wheedled himself a transfer to the Pacific. More fighting, more medals. He came home a hero. They said he was the bravest soldier in the army, but I think he just liked to kill. He re-enlisted when Korea broke out. More of the same. In between, he knifed a man to death in a bar. Maybe there were a couple more, I'm not sure. When the Vietnam War started, his sons took over where he left off. The Slagels and the Jukes don't seem to care much one way or another about being Americans, but as soon as a war breaks out, they suddenly become patriotic. A couple of them were even over in Iraq during the first Gulf War and a few more during the latest war in Iraq. I hope you don't think I'm being too cynical, but I reckon they're all motivated more by bloodlust than by love of freedom and democracy."

D. C. Slagel's home was the biggest in the hollow, kind of an upper-class shack. D. C. himself was sitting on the porch cleaning his rifle. He must have been eighty-five years old, but he appeared as nimble and alert as a man thirty years younger. Beside him was a full-bodied woman in her forties. Voluptuous was the word that came to mind, although I had never before thought of it being applied to a woman that old. Like Lard's ladies, she was dressed in a thin cotton dress that begged to be ripped off. Despite my big-city sophistication, I was beginning to feel clumsy and naive in the presence of the women of Misty Hollow.

"That's his third wife," Doc whispered as we neared the house.

"What happened to the first two?" I asked.

Doc raised his eyebrows a couple of times, but didn't say a word. "Good day to you, Mr. Slagel," he said when we reached the porch.

"Good day to you, Doc. Who you got with you?" He stared at me not with the eyes of an old man, but with those of a hardened, sexually active criminal. The air of the hollow felt thick with the most primitive emotions. It almost reeked of sex and violence. It seems picturesque and racy to write about it, but experiencing it in person was not at all fun or exciting. I thought about various "sexy" ambiences I had been part of: dance clubs, college parties. Their sexuality had been leavened by romance and flirtation. This was different. I felt that at any moment this old man, who was literally older than my own grandfather, could point his rifle at me and rape me.

Doc Wilton rattled off my alleged academic credentials and my phony excuse for being in Calhoun County, while I put on my innocent young thing smile. When Doc was finished, there was a long silence while D. C. Slagel stroked his rifle and contemplated me.

"Nice and spunky," he said at last.

I decided that spunky women are not the first choice of rapists and I relaxed a bit.

"Get Miss Watkins a chair, Annie, and bring us some hoe cakes," he ordered his third wife.

Once I was properly seated, a touch of grandfatherliness entered D. C. Slagel's manner. "Annie's hoe cakes are real taste fetchers," he said. "So, what sort of supernatural tales are you interested in?"

"Oh, you know, ghost stories, haunted houses...flying children."

Neither D. C. nor Annie reacted to my mention of flying children. Instead, D. C. launched into a string of tales about weird voices in cemeteries, phantom lights in abandoned houses and unexplained footprints. I whipped out my trusty notepad and pretended to take notes. If I really had been a folklorist collecting supernatural tales of Tennessee, D. C. Slagel would have been the perfect informant. As it was, once it became clear that he knew nothing about a flying child, I quickly lost interest and became impatient.

As I listened to D. C. Slagel, I noticed a disturbing tendency in his speech. No matter what story he started to relate, he always seemed to end up telling me about a murder. "Back in 1860, a ten-year-old orphan girl was found dead, tied to a tree. Her ghost used to haunt the nearby cemetery.... In 1900, Martha Asher of Lone Mountain found out that her lover, Walter Luster, was actually married. She broke off their courtship, so he killed her. In the penitentiary he found Jesus and repented. Even nowadays when people go up to Lone Mountain they get a spiritual feeling by the spot where the girl died."

Exhilarated by the subject of murder, he went off on a tangent about all the sheriffs and policemen who had been killed in Calhoun County. I was sorry my brother wasn't there to enjoy the litany.

"A policeman named J. D. Criss was murdered in 1923 while he was tracking some moonshiners. Same thing happened to Sheriff Purslane Ellis two years later. Served them both right, interfering with working men trying to make a living....In 1962, constable Corning and his assistant Hunk, were killed in Happy Grove by a former deputy, Bud Dingus, and his cousin Ralph."

D. C. Slagel's monologue was punctuated by the arrival of a stream of relatives who were attracted by the news of an unexpected visitor. Lard Slagel arrived with his lusty sister-in-law. So did Lard's brothers, Lem and Lige, along with their wives, Prissie Juke and Loretta Juke. They were accompanied by a passel of younguns, aged about fourteen down to brand new. Various other cousins, aunts and uncles and so forth clustered around until D. C., Doc and I were surrounded by no less than twenty-three Slagels and Jukes spanning four generations. Each of the men carried a rifle, and several of them actually wore pistols strapped around their waists.

At one point I tried to shut up D. C. Slagel by saying, "This has been a most valuable session for me. I'm sure that many of your tales will end up in my thesis."

"Ooo, listen to her," exclaimed a huge, menacing roughneck in his thirties who turned out to be Armpie Juke. A deep scar stretched from his left temple across his mouth to the right side of his chin. "A real intellectual. Guess she'll be wanting to meet brother Judge."

I glanced over at Doc, who nodded to acknowledge that Judge Juke was another who, like him and Granny Slagel, had been given a name it would take a while to grow into.

"Why would I want to meet Judge?" I asked.

"He's the egghead of the holler," answered Lard. "Used to be pretty sharp, but he's been all fucked up since he come back from the I-Rack War."

"Before we go," interjected Doc, "do you want to ask your other question?"

"Sure," I said. "Do you know of any people around here whose homes are so remote that they can only be reached on foot?"

"What about that gro— uh, what's his name, that lives out toward Dark Mountain?" suggested Lem Slagel.

"You mean Weird Eddie?" answered Armpie. "No Jeep could get out where he lives."

"What's he like?" I asked.

"He gives me the creeps," answered Armpie. "I stay away from him."

I tried to imagine what sort of person would give Armpie Juke the creeps.

"Eb's been out to Weird Eddie's place," added Armpie. "Maybe we should take you over to talk to Eb."

"Fine with me."

Doc and I were then provided with what amounted to an armed

escort. All of the women and children vanished. Accompanied by Lard, Lem and Lige Slagel and Armpie Juke and his grizzled uncle, Goob Creech, we followed a back path over a hill and down into the sub-hollow inhabited by the Juke family. There were six more wood cabins, much like the Slagels'. I noted the same abundance of four-wheel drive Jeeps, but only one satellite dish. We walked right in front of four of the cabins, but no one came out to greet us, although I detected several sets of eyes peeping out of the darkness inside. Eb Juke's cabin appeared to have been constructed completely with recycled lumber. Some of the pieces were still covered with paint of various colors, others were natural, and still others bore the remnants of advertising posters. No attempt had been made to achieve a coherent pattern or design. As we approached, I could feel Doc Wilton become tense, his attention drawn completely to his lost love inside. Closer still, despite the clumping of my armed escort, I could make out voices raised in anger, men yelling and cursing. Instinctively I slowed down, not wanting to intrude on a family argument. But Lard, Lem, Lige, Goob and Armpie went straight up the front steps and through the front door without even knocking.

I followed them inside. The room smelled of molasses and buttermilk. A fat quail hung dead from a string on a nail by the stove. I sized up the situation as quickly as possible. A short, muscular man about my age—a man with handsome features, a rock jaw and clear blue eyes—was standing between a taller, somewhat older bearded man and a beautiful younger woman, fair skinned, her breasts filled with milk, a newborn resting in the crook of her arm. I surmised that the sparkplug in the middle was Eb Juke, the other man was his older brother, Judge, and the woman was Granny, the girl of Doc Wilton's dreams.

As we entered, Eb was screaming, "You keep your fucking hands off her!" and Judge was yelling back, "I didn't touch her!"

I looked more carefully at Granny Juke and noticed that her left cheek was burning red and her eyes were filling with tears. Armpie Juke, the embodiment of insensitivity, slapped his two younger brothers on the back and said, "What's happening boys? We brought you a little visitor."

"Are you all right, Granny?" asked Doc.

"Shut up, Dickhead!" said Eb.

Granny silently appealed to her three brothers and suddenly it dawned on Lem, Lige and Lard that gosh, gee, maybe something was wrong. Lem, the oldest of the Slagel boys, pulled out his gun and held it two inches from Eb Juke's nose. "Did he hit you, Sis?"

Granny nodded.

Eb was quick to defend himself. "If your wife was flirting with another man, you'd hit her too."

"I wasn't flirting. All I did was show sympathy to Judge. He's tormented."

"He was whining again about the goddamn Irackees," explained Eb.

"He's like a broken record."

"Jesus Christ," said Armpie, "when are you going to get over that damn war? It's old news."

"I can't pretend that I'm not haunted by what I did," said Judge. And, yes, by that one sentence alone it was clear that he was more intelligent than the rest of the Slagels and Jukes.

"Goddamn, Judge," said Lige Slagel, "you been back for three years. Can't you just get over it by now?"

"Did Uncle Rufus get over the Vietnam War in three years?" asked Judge.

That shut them up. The room filled with a heavy silence. I knew better than to ask about Uncle Rufus, but I was dying to know.

"Do you mind my asking what it is about the Iraq War that still upsets you?" I asked instead.

"Who's she?" asked Eb Juke.

It was Goob Creech who spoke up on my behalf. "She's an egghead like Judge. From North Carolina. She's writing about ghosts and hermits. D. C. told her a lot of tales, but she wants to know more."

This muddled summary of my cover story seemed to satisfy everyone, so I made no attempt to clarify my interests.

"She wants to know about Weird Eddie," added Armpie.

"Can I hear about the Iraqis first?" I asked quickly.

"Holy shit," mumbled Lem Slagel. He withdrew the gun from Eb Juke's nose and he and Eb and Lard and Lige and Goob retreated to a corner of the room, where Eb produced a jug of wine and passed it around.

"Won't you sit down?" asked Granny.

She led Doc and me to two chairs in front of a slab of wood that was laid on top of a box and that passed for their living room table. Judge Juke joined us.

I cooed over the baby for a while and then Judge looked me in the eye and said, "I buried alive about a dozen Iraqis."

"I beg your pardon?" I said. There was something vaguely familiar about Iraqis being buried alive, but I couldn't remember the details. The "Shock and Awe" invasion of Iraq seemed a distant passing fad, like Hula-Hoops or The War on Drugs.

"On the first day of the ground war it was my battalion's job to penetrate the trenches and bunkers that the Iraqis had set up as their first line of defense. We ordered them to come out and surrender, but they didn't, so we buried them alive. I was driving one of the bulldozers that covered them up. At the time I was hyped up with the fear of my own death, but when the war ended and I had time to think about it, it hit me something awful. Those were draftees down there in those trenches, kids who were torn away from their families and forced by Saddam Hussein to fight under penalty of death. I got to wondering why they hadn't come up. Maybe they were afraid we would kill them. Maybe it never occurred to them that we would bury them alive. I needed to talk about it, but nobody wanted to. When I got back home, there was a parade and everyone told me I was a hero. My family was proud of me. Some of the boys were even jealous that they didn't get to do some killing. But I couldn't stop thinking about those Iraqi boys and their families."

"They were just ropeheads," called out a voice from the wine jug corner of the room.

Judge Juke shook his head sadly. "They were human beings," he said quietly.

"I'm sorry," I said. "It must be hard for you here."

"It is!" interjected Granny, her eyes filling with tears again. It sounded like she meant it for both of them.

The wine jug boys left their corner and crowded around us by the makeshift table. I couldn't help but give them dirty looks.

"Mmmm, she's spunky, ain't she?" commented Lige.

"That's what I said," answered Lard.

"So what exactly is it that you want to know about?" asked Eb.

"Supernatural tales." I told him that D. C. Slagel had been a rich source of information and I paraphrased a few of the juicier ghost stories.

"Well, I'm sure none of us can add anything that D. C. hasn't already told you."

"There is one type of story I'm trying to track down around the state that Mr. Slagel didn't know anything about. By any chance, do any of you know anyone who claims to have seen a man or a boy flying through the air?"

I don't believe I've ever seen six drunk men sober up as quickly as did Armpie, Eb, Goob and the Slagel brothers. I knew instantly that I had hit the jackpot. Everyone in the room began exchanging looks. After a few seconds of silence, I noticed that the looks were settling on Armpie Juke, Lem Slagel, Goob Creech and Judge Juke.

"Might as well tell her," said Judge.

"No need," countered Armpie.

"It happened about twelve years ago," continued Judge. "Wasn't it? I was fourteen years old."

"Shut up, little brother, she could be law."

"I'm not law," I interjected, "and I promise not to use your names if I use the story in my thesis."

There was another agonizing silence. Then Judge Juke went ahead with his story.

"It was just before dawn. The sky was already lightening, but the sun hadn't popped up yet. Armpie was driving, Lem was riding shotgun, I was in the middle and Goob was in the back with the harvest."

"Hey," yelled Armpie and Lem simultaneously.

"She won't say anything, will you?" asked Judge.

"Cross my heart and hope to die. Besides, the statute of limitations has run out."

"It was an exciting day for me," Judge continued. "It was the first time I was allowed to go with the big boys on a run to Cincinnati. We had planned to leave much earlier, but the others had stayed up smoking the profits and drinking and before we knew it, it was almost sunrise. We'd only gotten as far as Double Death Creek— that's where Weird Eddie lives now, although he didn't at the time—when we saw a young boy flying through the air. Armpie yelled, 'Jesus, I just hit a kid!' Lem said, 'I didn't feel no bump, but I saw him too.' Armpie stopped the truck and said, 'Let's go find him.' Lem said, 'What, with 250 pounds of pot in the back?' 'We've got to,' said Armpie. 'He was a kid. I can't leave a *kid* to die."

I choked a bit at this disturbingly subtle moral distinction, but I managed to hide my reaction.

"We got out and searched the bushes by the side of the road, but we couldn't find anything," said Lem. "Not a trace. And we looked hard."

"It was the damnedest thing," added Armpie. "We looked everywhere, even under rocks. We couldn't find that kid. Then we thought maybe he had hobbled off, frightened like, so we spent over an hour combing the area, but we never even found a footprint."

"I know what you're thinking," said Judge. "We were all so stoned and drunk and tired that we couldn't see straight. But I was only fourteen, and I wasn't smoking or drinking and I saw it. And besides, for Armpie Juke to stop his truck with 250 pounds of marijuana in the back, you know it was serious. I'm telling you, that kid just disappeared. There's no explanation."

Of course, I knew what the explanation was, but I wasn't about to say. My heart was beating rapidly. It was all I could do to mask my excitement.

"What did the little boy look like?" I asked, as calmly as possible. "How old was he?"

"He was about ten years old," suggested Lem, "judging by his body. I couldn't make out his face, it happened so fast."

"I think he was younger," said Judge. "I caught a glimpse of his face, just for a split second. I think he was a really husky eight-year-old."

Eight plus twelve, I thought, exactly right. I was straining to keep my secret.

"I know you said there was no explanation, but looking back, what do you think happened?"

"Ghost," said Armpie Juke.

"One of the Double Death ghosts," agreed Lem Slagel.

"Huh?"

"Didn't D. C. tell you about the haunted house at the head of

Double Death Creek?"

"Yeah, he did," said Doc.

It must have been when I wasn't paying attention, I thought. "Sure, he did," I said, "but he told me so many haunted house stories that they kind of ran together. Tell me again in your own words."

It was Goob Creech who leaned forward to narrate the story. "You know, most haint tales go back to the turn of the century or even to the Civil War, but this one's different. Double Death Creek used to be called Bear Creek because onced upon a time there used to be a family of bears living up there. Just before the Second World War a family moved up the creek and built a house. They were called the Russells, and they come down here from Monroe County up in Kentucky. They raised a bunch of kids and all the kids moved away and by about 1960 all that was left was the man and his wife and their youngest, an eleven-year-old boy. I was twelve years old then and I knowed him—Little Charlie. Nice kid, never mean to no one. One evening Little Charlie's daddy, Bo Russell, walked into a beer joint up in Irma Springs. My daddy was there when it happened. Bo seemed more crazy than usual, talking strange and stuff. Had a couple of drinks and then, out of the blue, says, 'Well, I shot my wife.' They'd had an argument. Not about sex or money, just sick of each other. So he shot her and killed her. Nobody said nothing. Then Hogface Goad said, 'What about Little Charlie?' Bo Russell burst into tears and said, 'I killed him, too. Didn't mean to. He rushed at me yelling, "Pa, please don't shoot Ma!" My trigger finger had already moved and Little Charlie got in the way.' Then he cried some more. Then he stopped suddenly, pulled out a pistol and blew his brains out. Some of it landed right in my daddy's beer."

I was so absorbed by this appalling chronicle that I was momentarily distracted from the excitement of my quest. Hogface Goad? And Bo Russell's brain landing in Goob Creech's father's beer?

"The bartender gave him a free glass on the house," Goob added, matter-of-factly. "The other Russell kids come back and buried their parents and Little Charlie. Two of the brothers moved into the house, but they kept seeing Little Charlie's ghost leaping through the air, so they moved out. No one's gone near the house since. When Weird Eddie announced he was gonna build a cabin up Double Death Creek and start growing, we warned him about the haint, but he said he wouldn't go that far up the creek, and besides maybe the law would be too scared to go searching around a haunted place."

In a flash, it all came to me. If Tom and Tammy wanted to hide in a place where no one would find them, what could be better than a haunted house at the top of a remote creek.

"Weird Eddie still lives there?" I asked.

"Yup."

"Anyone else live up Double Death Creek?"

"There used to be a crazy old guy who lived beyond Weird Eddie," said Armpie, "a hermit. He used to appear on the road every few months and thumb a ride into town. He used to talk to himself and giggle a lot."

"Haven't seen him in years," added Lem.

"Probably died up there," suggested Lige.

I turned to Doc Wilton. "How did you handle Double Death Creek when you did the census?" I asked.

"I wouldn't go near the place. It wasn't the haunted house I was afraid of, it was Weird Eddie. I counted him as one Caucasian male, aged about thirty, figured the old hermit was dead and left it at that." After a few seconds of silence, Doc added, "We'd better get going. The sun's going down and I'd rather not get caught on that road after dark."

Lard Slagel stood up. "If you've got any more questions, honey, you're welcome to spend the night at my place."

The other boys hooted. "I reckon you're not her type," said Lem. "Maybe she'd rather stay with Judge."

"Thank you for the invitation," I said, as politely as I could, "but I have a lot of work to do." There was a flurry of farewells. When the leave-taking ritual was played out, Doc Wilton, hands in his pockets, said softly, "Goodbye, Granny. Please take care of yourself."

"Thank you, Doc, I'll do my best."

"Shove off, Dickhead," said Eb Juke.

As we walked back to the car I tried to cheer Doc up. "She likes you, Doc, I can tell. Someday your time will come."

"No it won't. If she ever leaves Eb, she'll just move on to Judge."

I felt bad for Doc. It was depressing to walk beside him. "Can I ask you a question?"

"What?"

"What happened to Uncle Rufus?"

"Who?"

"The one who didn't get over Vietnam."

"Oh, you mean Rufus Creech, Goob's brother. I guess he was pretty nuts to begin with, but when he got back from the Vietnam War, he was out of control, picking fights, screaming in his sleep. Evidently he'd seen or done some pretty bad things. But he wouldn't talk about it. A few years later, a friend of his dared him to put a stick of dynamite in his mouth and light it. He did it. Not only did he kill himself, but his parents, who were sleeping in the next room, were blown to pieces too."

I was sorry I had asked. I had thought New York City was a violent place, but Misty Hollow made the South Bronx look like Mister Rogers' neighborhood. We drove back in silence, but after a mile or so Doc pointed off to the left and said, "That's Double Death Creek."

I put my hand on his arm and said, "Wait a minute."

Doc stopped the car and I stared into the forest. Up there lived Tom and Tammy and their flying child. At least they had been there as recently as twelve years ago. I was sure of it.

I hope you're not thinking of going up there," said Doc.

"Why not?"

"Weird Eddie would shoot you on sight. He's growing marijuana in there and he doesn't take kindly to trespassers."

I couldn't keep my eyes off the spot where the trickling water disappeared around a bend. "Why do they call him Weird Eddie?"

"One time when he was about thirteen, he caught a rattlesnake, strangled it, bit off its head and ate it."

"I see. Well, that explains it."

"Then he raped a blind girl and they sent him away until he was eighteen. Two weeks after he got back, he raped his grandmother. He went to prison for five years. When he returned, he had the good taste to move as far away from other people as he could get."

"I guess I won't make a trip up Double Death Creek, after all," I said. But I knew I really would.

Doc Wilton invited me to dinner, but I told him I was too tired. I picked up an awful chicken salad sandwich to go and sat in my room, analyzing the day's revelations: the eight-year-old boy flying across the road, the house up the creek that no one would go near. I couldn't wait to hike up the creek. And yet there were clearly serious dangers involved. The warnings I had received weren't just the product of someone's overactive imagination. Even if I could ignore the rattlesnakes and the ghost of Little Charlie Russell, I would have to find a way to deal with Weird Eddie. Still, I couldn't stop now. I was too close. A human being who could fly. I went to sleep imagining my acceptance speech at the Pulitzer Prize awards banquet.

The next day I slept late and then drove into Knoxville, which was sixty miles from Kilgore. I stopped at a sporting goods store and bought a backpack, a sleeping bag, waterproof hiking boots and all the other accessories needed for an overnight hike in the mountains: groundcover, flashlight, Swiss army knife, etc. Then I went to an electronics store and bought a camcorder and three blank cassettes to supplement the camera I always carried with me. Finally, I stocked up on food supplies: bread, cheese, peanut butter, bottled water. I remembered a detective story I had once read in which the bad guy, a robber, had slipped by a vicious guard dog by feeding him a slab of raw meat. So I had the butcher cut up a two-pound piece of prime rib and wrap it inside a couple of plastic bags, just in case Weird Eddie had a guard dog. In fact, it sounded like it might be worth trying on Weird Eddie himself.

I was not an expert at camping out, but I did have some experience. Of course there was that night I spent with the two sheriffs in Colorado, waiting for the cow carcass to disintegrate. But there was also a longer expedition I once made in New Mexico. Residents of the small village of Tequin had noticed that the water in the Sangre de Cristo Creek that passed through their town was turning red. Naturally, they were disturbed, but, given the name of the creek, they were also thrilled. I was fortunate in this case to have been notified by telephone as soon as the water changed color. I arrived in time to join a group of eight hardy locals who had volunteered to trek to the source of the stream. It took us three days. I had suspected that the blood of Christ was really going to be some form of industrial or agricultural pollution, but in fact it turned out to be something more unusual. A small earthquake, not felt in any populated areas, had cracked open a cave that was inhabited by several hundred bats. The soil of the cave had spilled out and was flowing into the creek. Our group was confronted by a sensitive moral dilemma. How should we break the news to the faithful folks down below that the blessed miracle water that they were now drinking and bathing in, the blessed blood of Christ, had actually been turned red not by divine intervention, but by bat guano?

Curiously, the agnostics on the trip wanted to report that no explanation could be found, but the two members who were representatives of the Catholic Church insisted that the truth be told. In the end, a compromise was reached. We reported that sediment from some rocks had leached into the soil and then into the stream. Of course when I got back to New York and wrote up the story, I couldn't resist telling the truth. I hoped my article never reached Tequin. At any rate, my five nights of camping out in New Mexico had given me confidence that I could backpack on my own in Tennessee.

Before I left Knoxville, there was one more thing I had to do. I had to take care of Doc Wilton. I was afraid that he would track me to Double Death Creek and try to follow me. It was important to me that I go alone. I suppose part of it was sheer stubbornness, wanting to prove that I, a woman, could do this by myself. But the primary reason, I am sorry to admit, was that I wanted the scoop all to myself. If there really was a young man who could fly, I wanted all the credit for discovering him. My plan was to videotape him in flight, interview him and then release the tape and the article simultaneously, making both of us international celebrities. If Doc Wilton tagged along, it would spoil everything. So before I left Knoxville I wrote a letter to Doc explaining that I had to leave Kilgore suddenly because of a family emergency. I dropped the letter in a mailbox near the Knoxville airport.

Back in Kilgore I parked my Chevy Malibu two blocks from the

Kilgore Inn and paid my bill before returning to my room. I spent the rest of the evening packing and re-packing my backpack. Then I set my wrist alarm for 4:00 A.M. and went to bed.

CHAPTER 8

DOUBLE DEATH CREEK

When I awoke it was still dark. I walked to my car and then drove east. When I reached the Selma Road, I turned off and retraced the route Doc Wilton had taken the day before. It was tough going in the dark, especially so because I kept my lights on low beam so as not to attract too much attention. After I passed through Misty Junction, the road got so bad that I had to slow to a snail's pace. The day before, I had noticed an abandoned railroad track about a half-mile north of Double Death Creek. I found it in the dark, bumped my way off Misty Creek Road, and hid the Malibu in a thickly wooded area about two hundred yards away. Then I shouldered my backpack and hiked up the road until I reached the point where it crossed Double Death Creek.

By this time the sun was starting to rise. As I stood at the spot that I had chosen as my trailhead, I experienced a pang of doubt. Behind me was civilization: telephones, televisions, warm showers, hot food, a good job, nightclubs, parties with witty repartee. Ahead of me was the unknown: rattlesnakes, bears, the skeleton of a hermit, a haunted house, a crazed marijuana grower who was prone to raping women and, if I was lucky, a family that didn't want to be found. If I turned back now, no one would know the difference. I had even brought with me from New York a research packet on the famous Kentucky meat shower of 1876, which I had planned to write about if the story of the flying boy didn't work out. If all I wanted from this quest was glory, I knew it wasn't worth it. No amount of praise and fame was worth risking my life for. No, here on the edge between safety and danger, I knew it was something deeper that impelled me. It was the dream of recapturing the innocent years of my early childhood, when everything was magic and even I could fly. I took one last look up the rutted road that led back to my car and to the city and to the airport and to my centrally heated apartment in New York City. Then I quickly turned around and plunged into the forest that guarded the entrance to Double Death Creek.

A simple, overgrown footpath ran alongside Double Death Creek, but I chose to hike as much as possible in the water so as not to leave footprints. At first I pushed upstream as quickly as I could, but after forty-five minutes the peaceful scenery lulled me into a more leisurely pace. The rising sun revealed a grove of hickory trees, then another of white pine. A rabbit hopped across my path. Evidently shocked to see an outsider, it stopped three feet away and stared at me for a good fifteen seconds before hopping away. A little farther on I surprised a family of deer that had come to the stream for a morning drink. I spotted a patch of yellow and discovered lady's slipper orchids.

By now, I had slowed to an amble. If it was reminders of my childhood that I was after, I couldn't have come to a better place. I lapsed into a nostalgic reverie, recalling the fantasies I had created on solitary walks when I was five and six years old. Back then I used to imagine that I understood the languages of the animals, like Dr. Doolittle. I used to engage in wonderfully affectionate conversations with squirrels and birds and spiders. I would imagine that I had wandered into a hidden kingdom and that the king and queen fell in love with me and invited me to be their one and only princess.

About an hour and a half after I had entered the wilderness, I was startled out of my reverie by the sudden appearance of a wild turkey and her four baby turkeys. I had never seen anything like it. They were so adorable that I vowed never to celebrate Thanksgiving again.

Lost in a blissful appreciation of nature, I was unprepared when a cold piece of metal was jabbed behind my right ear. I heard the click of a trigger and I felt my heart stop beating.

"Turn around," said a gravelly voice that sounded like it hadn't been used in months.

I turned around. Before me stood a truly evil-looking man. He was about six foot two and overflowing with muscle and fat. His head and face were freshly shaved, his nose was twisted, and his wild eyes were scarier than D. C. Slagel's. For twenty-four hours I had been having nightmarish visions of what Weird Eddie would look like. Unfortunately, he looked worse. I tried to smile and say something spunky, but when I opened my mouth my vocal cords went on strike. Even my saliva was hiding out somewhere. Weird Eddie did not have the same problem. He was drooling so heavily I thought a puddle would form between us. He poked me in the breast with his rifle and growled, "Let's see what you look like."

This brought me to my senses. Fortunately I was prepared for this threat. I fell back on a ploy I had used successfully twice before, once in a stairwell in Pontiac, Michigan, and once in a parking lot in Miami. I took a deep breath and started talking fast. "I'll bet you want to have sex with me," I began. "Well, that's not necessarily something I want to avoid, you being such a strong..." I tried to say "handsome," but the word got as far as my larynx and turned and went back down. "...such a strong, strong man. But there's one problem: I have AIDS."

"You're lying."

"I wish I was. In my backpack I have the certificate to prove it."

"Let's see it. And don't try any funny business."

A friend of mine at a medical laboratory provides me with a new set of fake test results and a bogus certificate every three months. I fished them out of my pack and handed them over to Weird Eddie. He read the papers very slowly and then his shoulders slumped in disappointment.

"Tough break," he mumbled as he gave the papers back to me.

"Yeah," I said, "the doctors say I only have a few more months to live."

"Huh? Oh, yeah, I guess it's a tough break for you too."

I was a bit irritated that he would rate the tragedy of my impending death *almost* on a par with his missed chance to get laid, but I let it pass.

"Well, I'd best be getting on," I said lightly.

"What are you talking about?"

"I want to get as far upstream as I can before nightfall."

"Upstream? You can't go there."

"Why not?"

"It's too dangerous."

When a man who once killed a rattlesnake with his bare hands, bit off its head and ate it, tells you something is dangerous, you tend to take it more seriously than the average warning. At least I do. But then I remembered.

"Oh, you must mean the Old Man and the haunted house."

"The Old Man and the haunted house? Hell, no. I've never gotten that far and neither will you. You see that ridge over there?"

I looked upstream and located a rocky overhang above the right bank of the stream about two hundred yards away.

"Yes, I see it."

"If you go past that ridge, you'll die."

"I'm about to die of AIDS anyway; what difference does it make?"

"I've heard about AIDS. It's a bad way to die, but it's peaches 'n' cream compared to what'll happen to you if you go past that ridge."

"All right. What will happen to me if I go beyond that ridge?

"Weird Eddie'll get you."

I slowly turned my attention from the ridge back to the grotesque brute standing beside me.

"You're not Weird Eddie?" I asked in a tone of voice that was pathetically meeker than the calm and collected tone I had planned.

"Hell, no! My name's Biff. Weird Eddie rents me out a patch of land to grow weed on and I give him half the profit. But he won't let me or nobody else go past that ridge. Nosiree, that Eddie is one mean son of a bitch."

Several thoughts flashed through my mind at that moment, all at once. Biff, who stuck a gun behind my ear and wanted to rape me, thinks Weird Eddie is "one mean son of a bitch." If I go past that ridge I will die a death worse than AIDS. Why was it I wanted to go upstream? To investigate a wild rumor that a young man can fly? Surely the prospect of fame, fortune and career advancement wasn't that important.

It is a sign of how deeply I felt my spiritual crisis that, after only a few seconds hesitation, I decided to press on. I looked Biff in the eye and said, "If I see Weird Eddie, I'll tell him you told me not to go. That way he won't blame you."

I turned and continued upstream. Biff was speechless for a bit.

Then he burst out with "But you'll die."

I stopped and faced him once more.

"We all die eventually."

Biff shook his head in awe. I swaggered on, greatly impressed by my own courage. However, as soon as Biff was out of sight, my knees began to quiver, my heart began to pound and I had to sit down to keep from fainting. I pulled my phony AIDS papers out of my pack and stuck them in my shirt pocket. This revived my confidence enough to allow me to resume walking upstream.

But when I got to the ridge I hesitated. Instinctively I looked left and right as if I was trying to cross a busy highway. I forced myself to plunge forward without further reflection. I took a few steps and was overjoyed to discover I was still alive. I scanned the ridge: no Weird Eddie. I looked upstream. Nothing. I listened for ominous sounds emanating from the trees or from behind the boulders. All was peaceful. It occurred to me that even if Weird Eddie was as evil as Biff had implied, he couldn't stand guard all day long. He had a life to live, illegal drugs to cultivate, rattlesnakes to decapitate. He was a busy man. Maybe I could pass through his domain without attracting his attention. I continued at a brisker pace. Every few seconds I checked behind my back, actually walking around three hundred and sixty degrees to make sure I wasn't being followed or watched.

Finally, I relaxed enough to realize that I was covered with fear-inspired perspiration. I looked around once more, listened carefully, and then took off my pack and put it down on a flat rock. Then I knelt down by the stream and scooped water over my face and neck. Suddenly I sensed that I was not alone. I jumped and turned around, my heart almost pounding its way out of my body. I saw nothing. My blood was rushing so fast I could hear it. After a few seconds I calmed myself enough to listen, but all I heard was the stream and a bird. I turned back to the water and watched as it exploded. From out of a waterspout, a human figure burst forward and grabbed me by the neck.

My whole body turned to liquid. He had the eyes of Charles Manson and the intense composure of Hannibal Lecter. I almost fainted, but he held me up. He was tall like Biff, but leaner. He had a long hollow reed sticking out of his mouth and a rifle slung over his shoulder. The hand that wasn't holding my neck held a very sharp hunting knife that he now raised before my eyes and then pressed against my neck.

"Take off your clothes," he said, allowing the reed to drop to the ground.

"I have AIDS," I said, so quickly that I amazed myself. "I can show you the certificate that tells how long I've been contaminated."

"Take off your fucking clothes."

"I said I have AIDS."

"What's that?"

I was not prepared for this. In all my travels in Yokelland, I had never met anyone who hadn't heard of AIDS.

"You know, Magic Johnson, Rock Hudson."

"Who?"

Now I was really starting to panic. "It's a disease that's transmitted during sex of any kind. It kills everyone who gets it. The doctors say I have less than a year to live. If you have sex with me, you'll die too."

"Bullshit. Take your clothes off or I'll kill you first and then fuck you."

"All right, all right, I'll do it. But there's one more thing you should know... I'm a lesbian."

A look of absolute fear transformed Weird Eddie's face. "You mean, you do it with girls?"

"Exactly. Other girls and I have a great time together."

Weird Eddie shrank from me like a giant afraid of a mouse. "I don't want to hear about it," he whined. "Don't say another word about it. And don't touch me."

I reached up and gently pushed the hunting knife away from my neck. Weird Eddie pulled the knife away and wiped the tip of it in the soil. "Just my luck," he moaned. 'The first piece of ass to show up out here in seven years and you're not even a real girl."

"Sorry, Eddie."

"How'd you know my name?"

"The Jukes and the Slagels told me. I wanted to go camping up this creek and they told me I'd better clear it with you."

"Didn't they warn you about the haunted house."

"Yes. Have you been up there?"

"Not a chance. I don't need no trouble."

"Anybody else live upstream?"

"Just the Old Man, but he's crazy."

"He's still alive?"

"As far as I know. I saw him about a year ago."

"Listen, by any chance, have you ever seen anything unusual flying through the air since you've lived on Double Death Creek?"

Weird Eddie looked at me, how can I put it—weirdly. "Sure have. Seen it at night a couple times and once at dawn. First time I thought it was a space creature, an alien. But the next time I realized it was a huge bird, big as a big man."

"When was the last time you saw it?"

"Five years ago. I took a couple shots at it. Don't think I got it, 'cause I never found its body, but I never saw it again."

Five years ago. I was so excited that I grabbed my pack and turned upstream without thinking.

"Where ya goin'?" asked Weird Eddie.

"I'm going to keep hiking."

"Why don't you rest awhile? Come back to my place and I'll make you breakfast."

I was strangely touched by this grandmother-raper wanting to cook for me, but not enough to delay my quest.

"I'm sorry," I said. "I'm supposed to meet my *girlfriend* by Dark Mountain. She's coming over from the other side."

Weird Eddie shrank back again and let me go. I waved goodbye and began sloshing up the creek. Eddie waved and then called out, "You watch out for the Old Man; he might be dangerous."

Nice talk from a man who, moments earlier, had threatened to kill me and then rape me.

"Thanks for the warning," I said.

I hiked on all through the morning and the early afternoon with brief stops for food and drink. The countryside turned increasingly wild. The creek cut its way through thick brush. Sometimes I was forced to inch my way up the sides of moderate waterfalls. Once I slipped and fell into the water up to my waist. After reaching the top of a particularly turbulent waterfall, I brushed myself off, looked up and saw an old man sitting on a rock beside the stream about fifty yards away. He was facing the other way and didn't see me. He had long white hair and a long white beard and he was dressed in rags. As I drew closer I could see that he was doing nothing in particular, just sitting and looking at the water. When I got to within ten feet of him, I cleared my throat loudly, but the water was slapping against the rocks with such force that he didn't hear me. So I walked around and stood right in front of him. After a few seconds, he noticed my feet and looked up. He looked me directly in the eyes, but, to my great surprise, he registered no reaction whatsoever.

"Hello," I said as gingerly as I was able.

Still no reaction. I wondered if he might be blind and deaf.

"My name is Suzy. Do you live around here?" It sounded as stupid as Hawley Huskins asking me if I was just passing through, but it did the trick. The old man snapped out of his trance and his eyes bugged out of their sockets.

"Are you real?" he asked.

"Yes. Are you?"

The old man laughed. I expected him to be toothless but, in fact, his mouth was full of healthy shining white teeth. "I haven't seen a real woman up here since the Russell shack got a haint."

"Yes, I heard about that. Sad story about the woman and child dying. When was that, about thirty years ago?"

"Is it? I don't keep track."

"Is the house still haunted?"

"Far as I know, it is. I don't go up that way much. Haven't been in sixty moons or so. Every time I got close I heard voices and saw spirits moving around."

"Spirits? What kind of spirits?"

"Man. Woman. Husky boy."

I felt a shiver course through my body. I removed my backpack and set it onto the ground. Then I bent down and took a drink of water from the stream. I composed myself and got ready for the big question.

"Have you ever seen any of these spirits fly through the air?"

"Oh, yes," he replied without hesitation.

"Which one?"

"The boy."

I almost started crying. I had to pause to regain control.

"When was the last time?"

"Maybe fifteen moons ago. Just at sunrise. Looked like it had been out roaming around and it was going home to sleep before sunlight caught it. Just like a vampire."

"What did it look like?"

"Husky boy, like I say. Patched clothes, moccasins, no beard. Don't think it saw me."

"You've actually seen a boy flying through the air more than once?"

"Many times. Mostly long ago. It was littler then. Since it got bigger, I don't see it so much, but I did see it that one time about fifteen moons ago."

I was overcome with emotion. It was true. My journey hadn't been in vain. My dream was about to come true. Tears ran down my cheeks. I closed my eyes and surrendered myself to a wave of bliss. I wondered if this might be my two seconds with God finally come to pass.

"I sure have seen that boy flying around," the old man continued. "And that's not all. I've seen the devil himself fly by a couple times and onced I saw three angels chasing after him. And onced I saw a hippopotamus hovering above those trees right over there."

I opened my eyes. "A hippopotamus?"

"That's right. Amazing isn't it. Who would have expected to see a flying hippopotamus right here in Calhoun County?"

If this was God's message to me, I failed to appreciate His sense of humor.

"That must have been quite a surprise," I said. "Gosh."

The old man began to ramble about how God sent him presents: black mushrooms from outer space, messages written in the clouds, possums that "talked English." My own communications with the Deity seemed cheapened and degraded by his descriptions. I didn't want to hear anymore, so I tuned out.

I would continue up the creek: there was no point in turning back after having come this far. But my enthusiasm took a nosedive. I felt silly with my camcorder and my fantasies of fame and reward. Maybe if I caught a few frames of the flying hippopotamus, I could become a YouTube hero.

"What's the quickest route to the Russell shack?" I asked, interrupting the old man in mid-sentence.

He didn't seem to mind. "There used to be a path, but it's all overgrown. You might as well just keep following the creek. That way you'll get there for sure."

I hefted the backpack back onto my shoulders. It felt ten times heavier than when I had taken it off. "I'd better be going," I said. "It was nice talking with you. You were very helpful."

"Pleasure was mine, Missy. You watch out for that mountain lion family upstream. And if the spirits don't get you, stop by when you leave and tell me what you saw."

"Sure thing."

I took my leave of the old man with his cheery blessing ringing in my ears: "if the spirits don't get you..."

After one more hour of hard climbing, the sun set. I laid out my ground cover and sleeping bag in a small clearing twenty yards away from Double Death Creek. I made myself a peanut butter sandwich and contemplated the night ahead. What with snakes and bears and mountain lions and ghosts and visions of the numerous violent episodes I had heard about, I expected to stay up all night worrying and then doze after dawn. Instead I crawled into my sleeping bag and was out like a light in about three seconds.

I awoke with a start a few hours later. I thought I heard the flapping of wings and imagined that an enormous owl was hovering above me. I had great difficulty getting back to sleep. All I could think about were frightening images: Little Charlie Russell leaping in front of his father's gun, pleading "Pa, please don't shoot Ma;" Weird Eddie telling me to take my clothes off; Bo Russell's brain landing in Goob Creech's beer; Iraqis being buried alive by U.S. troops; the ten-year-old orphan girl tied to a tree; Uncle Rufus putting a stick of dynamite in his mouth and lighting it; Lard Slagel leering at me; my mother screaming at my brother, calling him names, while he drifted off into fantasy. Every sound unnerved me. I imagined a rattlesnake crawling into my sleeping bag, Weird Eddie having a change of heart about lesbians, escaped prisoners emerging from the bushes. After two or three hours I was saved by sheer fatigue and I drifted back to sleep.

At dawn, I was awakened by a scraping sound. In my dream

state, Weird Eddie and my mother were digging a grave. The scraping sound was caused by their shovels rubbing against rocks. I opened my eyes—and there was a raccoon staring at me from less than a foot away. I took this as an auspicious sign. The sun had barely risen when I started out again up Double Death Creek. It was very slow going. I doubt that I made more than three miles in two hours.

It was the smell that attracted me before I even saw anything: the unmistakable odor of wood burning. Treading softly, I left the stream and picked my way through the thick forest. Then I saw it: a modest cabin with smoke coming out of a chimney. Instinctively, I set down my pack, opened it and pulled out the past-its-prime rib. Sure enough, there was a rustling of branches and two Doberman Pinschers, their ears cupped and their teeth bared, bounded toward me. I fished the meat out of its plastic covers and threw it at their feet. The Dobermans stopped cold and leaped at the meat. As soon as they finished devouring their treat, I rubbed them behind their ears. Before long, we were good friends, although they did seem disappointed that I had nothing more to offer.

I heard a quick whistle. The dogs turned on their heels and raced back home. I crept closer until I had a clear view of the cabin. I hid behind a log and studied the layout. The cabin was built in the style that I had by now become used to: steps leading to a porch, door smack dab in the middle, big windows on either side. There was a well-tended clearing in front of the house. The clearing was lined with fruit and nut trees, as well as lilacs and rose bushes. On the whole, the place was surprisingly neat and orderly for a home that was so remote. My hiding spot was off to the side of the house, in a straight line extending from the porch. I heard voices coming from just inside the front door, but I couldn't make out the words.

A man and a woman appeared. It was hard to make out their faces because of the angle, but it seemed to me that they did bear a striking resemblance to one another. They were the same size and same weight and their gait and hand gestures were similar. They both had wheat-colored hair.

"Hunting," was the first word I was able to distinguish. The man bounced down the steps. In one hand he held a bow, in the other, a quiver filled with arrows. The Doberman Pinschers clambered after him. The woman watched from the porch as the man and the dogs disappeared into the forest beyond the orchard. Then she took hold of a basket and strolled over to an apple tree that was picked clean on the bottom, but which was still full of fruit on the upper branches. She was dressed in an ankle-length patchwork cotton dress. Although she appeared to be in her thirties, her figure was as trim as that of a teenager. She climbed a homemade ladder and began filling her basket with apples. But it was hard going. All the best ones seemed to be just beyond her reach. Finally she became frustrated and descended. She walked halfway back to the house and called out.

"Davy!"

A tall, muscular young man emerged from the cabin. I couldn't see his face, but his hair, worn shaggy, was lighter than that of the couple I took to be his parents. I strained to pick up their words.

"...nice apples up top of the tree ... help me with them?"

"All right, Ma."

Davy grabbed a basket and strode across the clearing to the orchard. He was wearing denim overalls without a shirt. It was the first time I had seen muscles actually ripple. He looked like a Norse god from the fairy tales of my early childhood.

When he reached the apple tree in question, he stopped and appeared to close his eyes. His fists clutched, his muscles strained. He seemed to be concentrating his energy. Then, without further warning, he rose straight up from the ground to a height of about eight feet. He hovered for a couple of seconds and then shot forward and up until he reached the upper branches of the apple tree.

I was so overjoyed that I burst into tears. My body shook, but I was able to keep silent. The depth of my response amazed me. I needed to believe in a miracle and here it was at last. I dried my eyes and watched. Davy was plucking apples with what looked like ease, although I could hear his grunts clearly, even though he was a good thirty yards away. His mother was looking on with an expression that mixed maternal admiration and concern. I fumbled with my pack and pulled out my camcorder, praising myself for having the foresight to load it with tape and a battery before I left the Kilgore Inn. By the time I got the camera out, Davy had filled his basket and was back down again. His mother handed him another one and said, "How about those over there?"

Davy walked over to a second tree. This time he was facing me. I zoomed my camera as close as it would go. I could see him clearly now. He had blue eyes, a slightly stubbed nose and a granite chin with a dimple. I turned on the camera and observed his pre-flight preparations. He closed his blue eyes tight, and a grimace distorted his handsome face. Muscles taut, cheeks flushed. Then he began to disappear from the frame. I recovered from the shock and followed him as he rose, hovered, flew and—how strangely mundane— picked apples. I could see him working up a sweat. Even so, he flitted around amongst the branches like a hummingbird. As soon as the basket was full, he flew away from the tree and landed on his feet beside his mother.

"Thank you, Davy. I'll make us some good pies."

"I'd like to go join Pa."

"All right, go ahead. You be careful."

"I will."

Davy strained again, rose, hovered and took off in the direction his father had gone. He moved faster than a man could run. Unlike Superman, who glided effortlessly, Davy kicked his feet like a swimmer and fluttered his arms like they were wings, occasionally taking a sort of breaststroke for added speed. After ten seconds, he was gone.

I turned off the camera and collapsed behind the fallen log. I was perspiring, as if I, too, had been performing feats of strength. When I looked out again, the yard was empty. I rewound the tape and watched a few seconds of what I had recorded. There it was, as clear as could be: a handsome young man flying through the air, no strings attached. This little cassette would fetch a high price from the television networks. I made a mental note to keep my still camera handy when he returned so that I would have something to accompany my *Insider* article.

Looking back on it, I find it disturbing that I shifted so quickly from a state of spiritual bliss to thoughts of commercial exploitation, but such is the life of a journalist. I had to devise a stratagem for approaching Davy and his parents. It wasn't enough to have photographs and video footage; I had to get them to tell me their story. Even if I hadn't been a journalist, I needed to know just because I was curious. How much of my speculation about "Tom" and "Tammy" had been right? And what about Davy? What was it like to grow up in complete isolation from everyone but his parents? And why was it still necessary to remain in hiding? Why didn't his parents trust him to keep his special power secret? For that matter, why had they never gone public and exploited it themselves? If these three people had gone to such lengths to keep hidden for twenty years, it was going to be a tough job to squeeze the story out of them.

Davy and his father were gone for three hours. Davy flew in slowly just below the tops of the trees. His father and the dogs followed close behind. I was able to snap several excellent photos, using the presence of the father as proof positive that Davy was hovering ten feet above the ground. After they had disappeared inside the cabin, I packed up my camera equipment and quietly retreated into the forest. I retraced my path for a half-mile, found a patch of soft ground near the creek and dug a deep hole using a small shovel I had brought along to dig waste holes. This time I covered my camera equipment in plastic and buried it. After packing the ground well and making mental notes about the spot, I returned to my hiding place near the cabin. I heaved my pack onto my back, took a deep breath and walked out of the woods and into the clearing in front of the cabin.

The dogs were lying on the porch. They lifted their heads, pricked their ears and sniffed. But, seeing that it was only me, their old friend, they dropped their heads onto their paws and returned to their naps.

I took another deep breath and called out in a cheerful voice, "Hello, there, anybody home?"

There was a long silence. Then "Tom" came out of the house and stood on the porch. He was holding his bow in his left hand and an arrow in his right. A few seconds later, "Tammy" emerged and stood by his side. They stared at me like I was the landlord come to evict them. For my part, I was speechless. If you stripped away his beard and her feminine softness, they had the same face. They were clearly not only brother and sister, but twins. I couldn't keep my eyes off them and they appeared to react the same way toward me.

The silence continued unnaturally until a banging sound came from inside the house, followed by the clatter of objects falling. "Tom" and "Tammy" looked quickly behind them and then turned back to me.

"What do you want?" asked "Tom."

I had trouble spitting the words out. "I was hiking from Misty Creek to Dark Mountain and I got lost. I didn't know anyone lived back here. I didn't mean to bother you."

Then Davy appeared. His parents gasped.

"Get back inside," ordered his father.

"It's all right," replied Davy. "I can handle it." He leaned against the door frame, wedging himself into an awkward position with his back against one side, one foot pushed against the other side and his left hand above his head, grasping the top of the frame.

His father turned back toward me again. "I think you'd better go back where you came from," he said.

"I'd rather not. I've come all this way. I really didn't intend to bother you. If you could just point me in the right direction..."

"I'll show her the way," said Davy.

Again his parents gasped. They looked terrified, so much so that I was almost tempted to reject his offer. Almost.

Davy walked deliberately down the porch steps and took hold of one of the straps of my backpack. "Let me carry this for you." He glanced at his parents, who seemed to relax a tiny bit. I let Davy take my pack off my back. But as he took hold of it, he suddenly looked worried. "You're traveling pretty light. I think you could use some fresh apples. Don't you think she could, Ma?"

Davy's mother hesitated, then went back into the house, fetched a large basket of apples and handed it to her son. Davy opened my pack and, to my surprise, poured about forty apples into the space that had been occupied by my cameras. Then he closed the pack and hefted it onto his shoulders. He smiled slyly at his parents, signaled me to follow him and headed in the direction he had gone with his father earlier in the day. I followed. I looked back once and caught on his parents' faces the sort of anxious expression one sees on a mother and father whose son is taking out the family car for the first time after earning his driver's license.

We trekked along, Davy leading and I a few paces behind, for fifteen silent minutes until we came to a small meadow, a sort of meadowlet, just above the creek.

"Can we rest a moment?" I asked.

Without answering, Davy stopped, surveyed the area, and settled down beneath a tree. He did not remove my backpack. Instead, he wedged himself against the tree trunk in the same peculiar way he had in the doorway of his cabin. I plopped down against a tree several feet away. A few awkward moments passed without a word. Having lived the past few years in New York, I felt uncomfortable with prolonged silences, so I spoke up.

"I'll bet you don't get too many visitors out here."

"You're the first one."

"Really? How long have you lived here?"

"All my life."

"It must get lonely with no one to talk with except your parents. How often do you go into town?"

"I've never been into town. My father goes every couple years, but my mother and I have never left the forest."

"How old are you?"

"Twenty."

"Wait a minute. You're twenty years old and you've never talked with anyone except your parents?"

"You're the first."

"That's not normal."

"I know. My parents have told me a little about the outside world, but they don't like to talk about it."

"But why have you stayed here? Why haven't you at least gone in for a visit?"

Davy paused. Then he said simply, "This is a land of many secrets." There was another pause and then he added, "My parents have their secret and I have mine."

I felt that a moment of truth had arrived.

"I think I know your secret," I said.

I expected him to recoil, but instead he reacted calmly. "I know you do."

I was unable to hide my surprise.

"I saw you in the bushes when I was picking apples. You were watching me with binoculars."

Binoculars. Thank God for his naivety.

"I hope you'll excuse me, but I was shocked to see a person flying."

"My parents say I'm the only one in the world."

"I'm sure they're right. What I don't understand is why you keep your power hidden. You could give public exhibitions. You'd be rich and famous. The whole world would want to know about you."

"That's the problem. If people found out about me, they'd find out about my parents, too. My parents and their secret."

"You mean the fact that they're brother and sister, that they're twins?"

This time Davy was so surprised that he almost jumped. "How did you know that?"

"By looking at them. It's obvious."

"It is? I didn't know."

"All right, I understand why you want to keep your power a secret, but why not go out in the world and pretend you can't fly? Who would know the difference?"

"Like Superman? I know about Superman because my father brought me a comic book once. Unfortunately, it's not so simple. I can fly whenever I want to, but there are also times when I take off even though I don't want to. It happens when I'm nervous or upset. If I went among people, I'd be flying all over the place, banging against roofs and ceilings."

"But you're not flying now. Here you are talking to a stranger for the first time ever. Surely you must be nervous right now."

"I am. That's why I filled your bag with apples—to weigh it down. And look how I'm sitting. If I leaned forward a couple inches, I'd be up in the air within seconds. This tree trunk is keeping me down."

"Your name is Davy, isn't it? I heard your mother call you."

He nodded. "And yours?"

"Suzy." Davy and Suzy: like two little children hiding in an enchanted forest. But I wasn't a child; I was a journalist. No matter how much I wanted to lose myself in Davy's miraculous world, I couldn't stop thinking like a columnist for the *New York Insider*.

"Davy," I began cautiously, "I want to be completely honest with you." Oh, the horrible ways of journalists. Dear reader, if you ever find yourself being interviewed by a journalist, do not believe anything that follows the words, "I want to be completely honest with you." We journalists are like politicians: we can only get ahead in our profession if we learn how to fake sincerity. Despite my sympathy with Davy and my rapidly growing attraction to him, I shamelessly launched into a mock confession.

"The truth is that I didn't just stumble on your cabin. I wasn't hiking to Dark Mountain. I was looking for you. I'm a university student from North Carolina. I'm writing a paper about supernatural tales of the old and new South. While I was doing research in Kentucky, I met a woman whose mother was the midwife who delivered you. The midwife kept your parents' secret, but on her deathbed she told her daughter about the little baby who flew through the air. It doesn't have anything whatsoever to do with what I'm writing about, but the midwife's daughter helped me a lot, so, in exchange, I promised her that I would try to find out what happened to that baby. I guess it was her mother's dying wish that her blessing be sent to that child. Now I've found you and I send you the dying blessing of the midwife who attended your birth."

Davy's eyes filled with tears. I felt embarrassed and guilty...but not so guilty that I felt compelled to correct my lie.

"I think you should tell this to my parents," said Davy. "I think they'd like to hear this."

"I'm ready when you are. But before we go back to the house, can I ask you a favor? Can you show me again how you fly?"

He took off my backpack and instantly floated six feet into the air. There was none of the sweating and grimacing of his earlier flights in the apple orchard. Apparently the strong emotions evoked by our conversation relieved him of the strain of physical effort. He took a few breaststrokes and shot up to treetop level. Then he flew into the forest and disappeared. A few seconds later he reappeared from a different direction. He hovered above me, and then floated down, landing on his feet with a smile on his face.

I leaped to my feet. "Take me with you!" I demanded.

His smile vanished. "What?"

"Take me with you. Please. I'll climb on your back." His

shoulders slumped. "I can't."

"Why not?"

"You're too late. When I was little, it was the easiest thing in the world for me to fly. No effort at all. I just thought about it and I was off, staring at baby birds in their nests, zooming downstream, two feet above the water, playing hide and seek with a bear cub. It was wonderful. But when I got to be twelve or thirteen, I began to tire. I couldn't go so fast; I couldn't stay up so long. Ever since then, my power has been going away, little by little. As recently as two years ago I probably could have carried you up into the sky, but now, except when I'm nervous and can't control myself, it takes all my strength just to get myself off the ground."

"Couldn't you try?"

"It won't work. I'm sorry."

"Please?"

He sighed deeply. "All right, but you're going to be disappointed." He leaned down and I climbed onto his back, wrapping my legs around his waist and my arms around his neck. He took a couple of deep breaths and then I could feel his muscles tense and strain. He grunted. He pushed off with his toes; he quivered and shook. He perspired. He took more deep breaths. It was thrilling to be pressed up against such a powerful body exerting such tremendous effort. But, alas, Davy was right: we never got off the ground. At last, he gave up and dropped to his knees. I climbed off his back. He was panting, head hung low, the very image of a defeated warrior. I felt guilty for having subjected him to such a humiliation.

"I'm sorry," I said weakly. "I should have believed you."

He was too exhausted to answer. After a minute or two he rose, picked up my backpack and signaled me to follow him again. On the way back to the cabin I studied his beautiful body and thought about how well-spoken he had been when we talked. He was by no means eloquent, but neither was he gross and primitive like the Slagels and the Jukes. I wondered if there wasn't more to his parents' secret than the fact that they were brother and sister.

Davy's parents were standing on the porch waiting when we returned. They looked angry and terrified. Davy removed the backpack, opened it on top and poured the apples into a basket. His parents watched with astonishment. He pulled a bucket of water off the porch and poured it over his head, his shoulders, his back and his chest. Then he dried himself with a nearby rag. At last, he looked up at his mother and father and said, "She knows."

"What does she know?" asked his father.

"She knows I can fly. She saw me picking apples this morning. She also knows that you're brother and sister. She says she could tell just by looking."

"Tammy" buried her head in her hands. "Tom" looked like he was seriously considering killing me on the spot.

"I think we can trust her, though," added Davy, just in time. "She's got something to tell you." He turned to me. "Go ahead."

Lying to an innocent twenty-year-old had been relatively easy, but an anguished woman and a potentially murderous man presented more worrisome challenges. I repeated the story I had told Davy, this time with the addition of numerous dramatic pauses. There were enough elements of truth in my tale—North Carolina, deceased midwife, her daughter's curiosity—that I was able to convince them of my honesty. Of course, what really turned the tables in my favor was the biggest lie of all: the deathbed blessing. Both "Tammy" and "Tom" melted when they heard that and "Tammy" burst into tears.

She composed herself, heaved a great sigh and then said, "My name is Deloris; my brother's name is Doyle. Won't you come inside? I'm just preparing dinner."

"Wait a minute," said Doyle. "How do we know she's telling the truth? How did you find us?"

I reached into a side pocket of my backpack, pulled out a legal-size envelope, and extracted the letter I had purchased from Hawley Huskins. I handed it to Deloris, who melted all over again.

"After I got to Kilgore, I was lucky," I explained. "I headed for the most remote corner of the county and stumbled into your backyard."

Deloris opened the envelope and read the letter inside. She shook her head. "Oh my, what a hard life we've had. You make one mistake and pay for it forever. Come on inside."

The inside of the cabin was as clean and orderly as the yard. The furniture was all handmade from local woods. There was one large living room that included the kitchen and dining area. After much prodding, Deloris finally allowed me to help her with the meal preparation. We made a salad of garden-grown vegetables and a soup of wild leaves and roots. Deloris cooked up a couple of cottontails. We chatted lightly about the beauty of the area and she asked me a few questions about North Carolina. At one point she started to question me about world events, but then she interrupted herself and said, "No, I'd rather not know."

It wasn't until dinner was served and the men rejoined us that the conversation turned serious. Doyle remained sullen, but Deloris seemed relieved by my unexpected visit.

"We've been alone so long," she said. "If you don't mind, Doyle, I'd like to tell Suzy everything she wants to know."

Doyle shrugged.

"Go ahead," urged Deloris, "Ask us anything." But before I could, she went on. "I'll bet you're wondering about Doyle and me. We've been celibate since the day Davy was born. It's been hard, but we took his birth as a warning from God."

"There is one thing I don't understand. Down here in the Misty Hollow area, it seems like there's lots of brothers and sisters who've had babies together. Why have you stayed hidden all these years?"

"It's true that that's why we settled here," said Doyle. "In case somebody did find us, they'd be more understanding. But we're not from this county. We grew up in Murfreesboro. Both our parents were professors at the university there: Middle Tennessee State. History and American Lit."

"My father teaches psychology at the University of North Carolina," I piped in.

"Really? Then you understand the atmosphere, the social expectations. When Mom and Dad found out Deloris was pregnant, they hit the roof. Mom was an anti-abortion activist. And here was her fifteen-year-old daughter going to have a baby."

"They lectured me day and night," said Deloris. "Called me a whore and a slut. Told me I had ruined their reputations and that they'd probably be fired. They demanded that I tell them who the father was, but of course I wouldn't. When I started to show, they kept me indoors and told the high school I had mononucleosis. They kept badgering me to tell them the father's name. They wouldn't let up. They said he should marry me, that it was his responsibility."

"A couple weeks before her due date," Doyle said, "Dad got drunk and threatened to kick her in the stomach unless she told him who the father was. I couldn't take it anymore, watching them abuse Deloris. So I told them it was me. I thought they'd die right on the spot. Mom threw up. Dad tried to attack me, but he was too drunk to do any harm. I grabbed Deloris. We stole my mom's car and we ran away that night. If you met Mr. Huskins and you talked to the midwife's daughter, you know what happened after that. After the midwife left, we packed up and left immediately. We couldn't go home, but all we knew was Tennessee, so we headed back across the border. For the first few months it was terrible. I did odd jobs while Deloris hid out in the forest with the baby. It was winter and a couple times we thought we would all die.

"One day I was washing dishes in a restaurant in Irma Springs and I overheard an old-timer telling a visiting cousin about this haunted house up Double Death Creek and how nobody would go near it. I hiked up here and found it. I was too worried about real problems to be bothered by ghosts. It seemed okay to me, so I went back for Deloris and Davy and we moved in. It's been almost twenty years now and no one's bothered us. The first year, I went into town every couple months, but once we got the hang of living on our own there wasn't so much need. Whenever I go into town, I take a different route each time and I try to change my appearance. But, even with those precautions, I'll bet I haven't gone in more than ten times total in eighteen years."

"Don't you miss civilization?" I asked.

Simultaneously, Doyle said, "No," and Deloris said, "Yes."

"If they found out about Davy," added Doyle, "they'd ruin him. They'd turn him into a freak, make him put on shows."

"It won't be long before there's nothing left to show," said Davy.

"Maybe then," responded his father.

Deloris wouldn't let me help with the dishes, so after dinner Davy and I went out on the porch and watched the stars. At first, he had trouble keeping in his seat—literally. He floated up to the roof and back down again. But as we chatted quietly, he was able to relax and stay put. Davy was filled with questions about the outside world. He wanted to know my opinion of television, movies, telephones, schools, big cities, none of which he had ever seen. It was startling to be sitting inside the borders of the United States and meet a native-born American who had never heard or seen a telephone, never been on a date, never been to church.

When we both became too tired and too self-conscious to keep talking, Davy offered to let me sleep in his bedroom, while he slept on the floor in the living room. Lying in his bed, I hoped that he would tiptoe into the room and join me, but he didn't. Despite my extreme fatigue, I had trouble falling asleep. There were too many vivid moments from the day to review. I had never met an incestuous couple before, but I was touched by the concern they had for one another. Doyle and Deloris had sacrificed their lives to protect their son from exploitation, while Davy had sacrificed his freedom to protect his parents from public exposure. I couldn't imagine either of my own parents committing a similarly selfless act.

The next morning Deloris fed me a huge breakfast: an omelet, fresh apple juice, fresh bread made from the seeds of a plant I had never heard of and a cup of hot acorn "coffee" sweetened with honey. She also packed me a lunch. Even Doyle seemed in better spirits. "Thanks for your visit," he said. "I guess I needed to talk." But then a look of concern crossed his face.

"I know you're going to talk to the midwife's daughter, but you won't tell anyone else about us, will you?"

This time when I lied to Doyle, I even managed to look him in the eyes. "Oh no," I answered, "I wouldn't do that. You can trust me."

Davy accompanied me back the way I had come for about two miles. It was a warm, clear, sunny day, the kind that New Yorkers dream about, yet don't know what to do with when they get one. When we reached the edge of the domain of the Old Man, Davy stopped. He set down my backpack and took my hands in his. He seemed to want to say something, but was too shy to do so. Earlier I had given him a piece of paper with my New York address. I had told him I was moving there from North Carolina to start a job.

"I hope you'll come and visit me someday," I said, "or at least write to me."

He looked at the ground and blushed. "Suzy, I'm sorry I couldn't take you flying."

"Oh, don't worry about that."

"No, I know it was a disappointment for you. For me too. For so many years I wished I was normal, so I could be free to go wherever I pleased. But now that my power is vanishing, I miss it. I'm sorry."

I let go of his hands and pulled his face down to mine and kissed him. He responded without hesitation and wrapped his arms around me. I closed my eyes and felt the strength of his embrace. Every passion I had ever thought I had for any other man seemed superficial as I lost myself in what was surely the most loving moment I had ever experienced. Our bodies fused. I felt lighthearted, as if I was floating in space. Suddenly it struck me: maybe this was it, maybe God had finally gotten around to me and was using this pure young man to cleanse me spiritually and put me on the right path. I opened my eyes to gaze at Davy. His eyes were closed and he, too, seemed lost in a peaceful ecstasy. I wanted to kiss his forehead so I pushed down on my toes to lift myself higher. But there was nothing to push against. I looked down... and saw the treetops below me.

"Davy," I whispered.

He opened his eyes, but saw only me.

"Look where we are," I said.

We both looked around. The forest stretched for miles in every direction. Birds flew below us. A small cloud drifted right beside us. We held each other tighter. A wonderful smile spread across Davy's face.

"Climb onto my back," he said.

When I was secure, he swooped down into the forest and followed the creek upstream, twisting and turning a few feet above the water. Like a child on a roller coaster, I felt giddy with excitement. At each turn I expected to see the king and queen from my childhood fantasies. A nestful of baby sparrows chirped at us. A sunbathing copperhead twisted his head to watch us go by. Two beavers looked up from their work and stared. Then we rose above the trees again.

Suddenly, the sunlight was so strong that I had to close my eyes. Yet I felt bathed in a pure white light. It was as if nothing else existed; as if I, as an individual, had disappeared and I had merged

with the universe. A bit of shade brought me back to my senses...
literally. I could feel the movement of the air against my face. I could
hear birds and then leaves rustling. I could smell the fragrance of
flowers and trees, and then with a deep breath, I could smell Davy
and feel his skin against mine. I opened my eyes and there he was,
with that wonderful smile still on his face.

Davy performed a slow 360-degree turn and returned us to
the spot where we had taken off. We settled to the ground and he
helped me put my backpack on.

"Thank you, Suzy. I guess you're what they call a 'doctor,'
because you heal people."

"You're the healer, Davy, not me."

I cried when he left. My joy was mingled with the depressing
prospect of returning to my normal life. I had to backtrack to find
the spot where I had buried my camera equipment. Digging it up
made me feel wicked and unworthy.

One thing I've learned about traveling is that the road back home
always seems less interesting than the journey to a new place. Part
of it, of course, is that you're retracing your steps instead of exploring
new ground. But another factor, I believe, is that the traveler is
absorbed with all she has already seen. My trip back down Double
Death Creek was not without incident. I ran into both the old
hermit and Weird Eddie. I told them that when I got close to the old
Russell place, I felt the presence of ghosts and heard them shrieking
and turned back in a hurry. I reached Misty Creek Road after dark
and was immediately surprised by headlights in the distance. I hid
behind a bush and watched as Lem and Lard Slagel bounced by in
a pickup truck without noticing me. It was pitch black by the time I
located my Chevy Malibu. All this time, through hours and hours
of hiking, I had barely noticed my surroundings. Part of the time
I felt that I was content for the first time in my life, that my flight
with Davy had pacified all the demons inside me. But for most of
the trek I was burdened by the weight of the camcorder and the still
camera inside my backpack and, an even heavier burden, by the
images inside the cameras.

My article on "The Flying Boy of Calhoun County, Tennessee," came to me so easily I could have written it in one draft as soon as I reached the car. I knew, too, exactly how to market the story. The video footage belonged to me. Lute Wisdom and the *New York Insider* could make no claim on it. I would sell the video to one of the television networks and get them to release it the evening before my article appeared. It wasn't hard news, but as human interest stories went, it couldn't be beat. Of course I would be betraying Davy and his parents, but it wouldn't be much worse than the way I had treated other people I had written about. I rationalized like mad. Thousands of people, maybe even millions, would be touched by spiritual enchantment when they saw the video and then read my description of flying through the air myself. And it wouldn't really be so bad for Davy and his parents. They would be released from their prison. Davy could become rich and famous; Deloris and Doyle could publicly repent and be forgiven.

I spent the night at a motel on the outskirts of Knoxville. In the morning I drove to the airport in time to catch an early flight to Atlanta that connected with another one to New York. When I arrived at JFK, I walked straight to the taxi stand. Out of the corner of my eye I saw two garbage collectors emptying a dumpster into a mobile trash compactor. I opened my suitcase, removed the videotape of Davy flying in the orchard and the memory card with the photos of him hovering above his father. I fingered them lovingly, knowing that they could bring me financial security and international fame. With a sigh, I walked over to another dumpster and quickly flung the videocassette and the memory card inside. Then I watched as the garbage men attached the dumpster to the compactor. I listened to the crunching of plastics and metals and then caught a cab home.

On the street I stopped at a kiosk and bought a postcard of the Statue of Liberty. I addressed it to Helen Poltrain in Mosquito Lick, Kentucky. Then I wrote, "It's true." I put a stamp on the corner, popped it into a mailbox and walked back to my apartment. When I got inside I called up Lute Wisdom. "The flying boy lead didn't pan out," I explained. "I'll have the 'Kentucky Meat Shower' piece on your desk in the morning."

EPILOGUE

I never saw Davy again. However, two years later I did receive a letter from him. He had lost completely his ability to fly. Together with his parents, he had visited his grandparents, who had since retired and mellowed out considerably. They were so happy to have their children back and so delighted to have a grandson, that they forgave Deloris and Doyle.

Deloris had moved to Atlanta, where she was working as a grocery checker and going to night school, studying to be a veterinarian. Doyle had a job as a long-haul truck driver. For all his complaints about the outside world, he wanted to see as much of it as he could. Davy, like his father, wanted to sample life's simple pleasures, like nightclubs, fast foods and motorcycles.

As for my family, my father finally left my mother. She refused to grant him a divorce, so he lives in Durham out of wedlock with a former teaching assistant. My mother still lives in Timberlake and still insists that she was right about everything after all.

My brother lives in Winston-Salem. He married a tough gal from Philadelphia who works as a waitress while he stays home with their son. Kyle hasn't had a breakdown in six years, which is a record for him. Actually, as much as I like his wife, I think it was the internet that turned Kyle around. Collecting murders became so easy that to satisfy his collector's passion, he had to specialize. He created a web site that catalogued cases in which police officers and sheriffs had been killed in action. Because he included details of each case and a short profile of each victim, he attracted the attention of the law enforcement community, and he gave interviews and was invited to functions. Then they discovered that Kyle operated a second web site. This one details cases in which unarmed people have been killed by the police. He lost favor with one constituency, but gained the appreciation of another.

Of course, for me, the internet was also a game-changer. There is still nothing like interviewing people in person where they live and flourish. But, despite all of its fake stories and scams, the internet has been fantastic for leads and, if you know what you're doing, fact-checking, and for doing pre-interview research. As for the rest of my life, I still write my column for the *Insider*, but I also have my own podcast. I don't have a steady boyfriend, but there are a couple guys I see on a regular basis. The only person I ever told about my experience with The Flying Boy of Calhoun County Tennessee was Kyle.

The other day, I interviewed two brothers in Poughkeepsie who insisted that God had spoken to them on an unused channel of their satellite television system. They claimed that the Almighty had ordered them to devote their lives to getting everyone in the world to build statues of Jesus out of everyday household objects. I thought about my moments above the trees with Davy. If only these two silly people could know what it was really like to be visited by God. I felt suddenly sad, as if the highlight of my life had already taken place and all I could look forward to was fifty years or more of anticlimax.

Back at my office I got out a pen and paper and made some calculations. If God spent one and a half seconds with each person He visited instead of two seconds, that would give Him time to revisit 368,179,200 people. With seven billion people on the earth, that meant my chances of getting a second chance were…

ABOUT THE AUTHOR

David Wallechinsky is the author or co-author of many books, including *The People's Almanac, The Book of Lists, Tyrants: The World's 20 Worst Living Dictators* and *The Complete Book of the Olympics*. He is also the founder and editor-in-chief of the government watchdog web site AllGov.com.

Curious about other Crossroad Press books?
Stop by our site:
http://store.crossroadpress.com
We offer quality writing
in digital, audio, and print formats.

Enter the code FIRSTBOOK
to get 20% off your first order from our store!
Stop by today!

www.ingramcontent.com/pod-product-compliance
Lightning Source LLC
Chambersburg PA
CBHW061255170626
46809CB00007B/2998